CW00481223

"At last . . . a book that answers every question you had about Conjure but were afraid to ask! Written in the folksy style that belongs to Starr Casas alone and jam-packed with easy to understand explanations, simple working instructions, and fascinating historical tidbits—*Old Style Conjure* is an absolute treasure. It's a must-read for every practitioner of the ancient arts— and a must-have for every magical library!"

> —DOROTHY MORRISON, author of *Everyday Magic*, *The Craft*, and *Utterly Wicked*

"This is Starr Casas's best work yet, revealing the secrets of Conjure that anyone can use to enrich their lives. Everything you need to know is fully explained. This is a handbook created to be used and cherished and passed on down from generation to generation."

> —ROSEMARY ELLEN GUILEY, author of *Guide to Psychic Power*

"Mamma Starr is the real deal and her works and words speak that truth. This down to earth, practical guide to Conjure is a book you will want to keep forever. Whenever I learn from Starr Casas, she transports me to a place where I see, feel, and hear what needs to be done to get it right. *Old Style Conjure* is a gift to the folk magic community."

> —JACKI SMITH, founder of Coventry Creations and author of *Coventry Magic with Candles, Oils, and Herbs*

"Starr Casas is a true national treasure. She is an authentic hereditary practitioner of Conjure, among the most potent forms of traditional American folk magic. A vast repository and staunch defender of rapidly vanishing American folk traditions, Starr Casas is the real deal and *Old Style Conjure* is her best, most complete and comprehensive work yet. This is a practical book, chockful of Starr's own formulas, rituals, and works. Read it and learn how to effectively use time-tested techniques of Conjure to better your life and achieve your goals. Starr also presents and explains the history and philosophy of Conjure. This knowledge will help you become a better, more effective practitioner of Conjure, but it will also teach you much about the history of the United States. To learn from Starr is to learn from the source. Anyone seeking to comprehend Conjure and benefit from its powerful magic would do well to read *Old Style Conjure*."

—JUDIKA ILLES, author of *Encyclopedia of 5000 Spells, Encyclopedia of Spirits, The Big Book of Practical Spells*, and other books of magic.

"*Old Style Conjure* is written in Starr Casas's uniquely heartfelt and down-home conversational style that reads like you're getting advice from your best friend. With her lifetime of conjure work, Starr guides you through the roots, recipes, and rites of this powerful practice that is the legacy of those first Africans to come over on the slave ships—ancestors that conjure workers uplift and honor for both their sacrifice and their magic. With these tools, you will learn the ways of Southern magic that have been used by both black and white practitioners for centuries—steeped in African wisdom, the spirits of the natural world, and the strength of the Bible—itself a most powerful spell book in the hands of the true Southern Conjurer. If you want to learn the old ways of Southern Conjure from a true expert who has lived it her entire life, then look no further than Starr Casas!"

—CHRISTIAN DAY, author of *The Witches' Book of the Dead* and co-owner of Hex: Old World Witchery.

"Written by one of the most authentic practitioners of our time, *Old Style Conjure* by Starr Casas is incredibly rooted in the power of the Old Ways, while at the same time bringing a great deal of relevance and instruction for modern people. This book is a 'must have' for those who want to learn more about the inner practices of Conjure."

—RAVEN GRIMASSI, author of *Old World Witchcraft* and *Grimoire of the Thorn-Blooded Witch*

"Respect, Responsibility, and Family . . . these three words resonate when I reflect on Starr Casas and the gift her knowledge and integrity are to our modern magickal culture. I love *Old Style Conjure*: it's fascinating, insightful, practical, and powerful, just like Starr."

—FIONA HORNE, author of *Pop! Goes the Witch: The Disinformation Guide to 21st Century Witchcraft*

OLD STYLE
CONJURE

OLD STYLE
CONJURE

Hoodoo, Rootwork & Folk Magic

STARR CASAS

Foreword by Orion Foxwood

WEISER BOOKS

This edition first published in 2017 by Weiser Books, an imprint of

Red Wheel/Weiser, LLC
With offices at:
65 Parker Street, Suite 7
Newburyport, MA 01950
www.redwheelweiser.com

ISBN: 978-1-57863-622-8
Library of Congress Cataloging-in-Publication Data available upon request

Cover design by Jim Warner
Cover photograph Rooster with basket-like comb (*Gallus gallinaceus crista in calathi modum efformata*), colour etching by Lorenzo Lorenzi and Violante Vanni, from *Natural History of Birds* by Saverio Manetti (1723-1784), Florence, 1767–1776
Interior by Maureen Forys, Happenstance Type-O-Rama
Typeset in Goudy Old Style and Windlass

Printed in Canada

MAR

10 9 8 7 6 5 4 3 2

To all the ancestors who suffered and survived and whose blood, sweat, and tears made this work possible! I honor you with every word I write.

CONTENTS

FOREWORD

Magic Remains

An ancient voice within our blood beckons, come to life!
It speaks of freedom to create and banish blight and strife.
When hope and law and prayers fail to thwart the haters harm,
It's magic that will set it right with candle, smoke, and charms.
When the money bird has left our nest and lack assumes its throne,
The door of magic opens wide when first we read the bones.
Roots and conjure, spirits and flame, the magic wears so many names.
From old world to new world to worlds far beyond,
Freedom from tyranny remains as our bond.
By crossroads and candle and cauldron and flame,
The spirit of magic shall always remain!

THE PRACTICE OF MAGIC and the use of divination to inform it are central and respected traditions in all ancient civilizations worldwide, and archaeological research will show that. This suggests that these practices have been important to hundreds of cultures over thousands of years of time and are more than mere superstitions or belief systems. They are a core component of the human experience at its very foundations. That alone should suggest to contemporary humanity that they are valid, helpful (even crucial), and sacred considerations based on the distilled wisdom of countless generations of experience. Yet their value and impact have also inspired a less-approving response in later generations, but specifically in religious and governance bodies who declared and executed what could be viewed as a war on magic! Proscribed as heresy and often scourged under the banner of witchcraft, it seems that magic was an enemy to convention, compliance, and conversion, and these tyrannical forces mounted severe attacks on its workers that lasted for hundreds of years. Yet, regardless of the looming threat of horrific sanctions, exiles, and the mass death sentences of the so-called "holy" inquisitions; *magic has not gone away . . . nor will it*. With that being said, our challenge is, as my dear friend the respected author Raven Grimassi would say, "to ride on the momentum of the past" through the needs, inspiration, and discernment of the present into a future that is healthier, happier, and more whole with the aid of magic.

It seems that the mysterious ways of magic will migrate, morph, erupt, and expand as it is needed and/or summoned and its worth is higher than the severity of the sanctions imposed against it. In fact, it seems that this mystical force and the art of shaping its outcome are most apparent and important at times of lack, need, and oppression. Further, its inherent worth grows muscle and volcanic velocity when freedom, justice, and equity are most challenged and restricted. Its inherent worth to the enduring human spirit is in its ability to grant power to the powerless, hope to the hopeless, and prosperity to the impoverished, while decreasing lack and increasing well-being. At the highest levels, the worker of magic may aim at the larger picture of reducing the presence and power of outrageous inequity. When magic blooms and its assistance is sought, the need for the magic maker or, in the parlance of this book, the rootworker or conjurer is greater than ever. The resources in *Old Style Conjure*, in my view, have arrived to empower the new seeker of sound magical practices and the seasoned worker alike with lore and practices that carry the power of the past to the need of the present.

It is a literary crossroads where old-style Conjure meets new-style life and magic continues to reach those who need it, the worker who works it. But for this gift to have the blessings of integrity as it is given, the story of Conjure's arrival in North America and the legacy of the African people who laid its foundations with their traditions and, yes, their lives must be acknowledged and honored. This is a core aspect of the ways of traditional, cultural, and folkloric magic, and Starr makes this clear in this book.

The worth of the conjuring tradition has many wonderful implications. On one hand, the recipes and practices Starr provides really work. I should know: I have applied works I've learned from Starr and their effectiveness was irrefutable. But, there's a deeper, more sacred virtue in how she delivers the traditional wisdoms of the practice. You see, while the work is addressing practical needs, it is also increasing the power of the worker (or their client) to achieve the ultimate expression of free will: choice over the shape of their destiny. Magic as a gift from the Creator, then applied by the worker, is an act of empowered choice to become a self-created being with the conscious power to choose one's destiny, a sacred core component imbued in humanity by God.

Magic, in my view, is the clearest expression of the biblical concept that we were made in God's image. Magic involves an interactive relationship with the creator force through the agency of prayer, incantation, ritual, gathered magical force, and the list of forms of magical practice goes on. So, what does magic, specifically "folk magic" and the variant known as Conjure, look like in the multifaceted subcultures of the United States? Well, Starr Casas has invited all of us into what she terms "the culture of Conjure," which includes a collective of lore, practices, and prayers passed on to her through family tradition, mentoring by elders, and an astute observation of practitioners, as she was honed and tested during the early phases of her life. But where does the body of this conjure tradition fit into the magical landscape of our country?

The United States is a hotbed of diverse folk magical traditions from many countries and cultures that made their way to its soil through colonization, migration, and the African slave trade of the 1700s and 1800s, to name some of the largest sources. But these influences were hardly the root of magic in the Americas, as that was already thousands of years deep in the soil of this land and flourishing, cultivated by the many indigenous tribes at least until colonialization aggressively sought their land, killed their people, and progressively eradicated many native peoples and their magical wisdom forever.

We will never know the sacred, powerful, and much-needed magical knowledge that was lost. Still, some of teachings and practices are preserved in the body of conjure practices, as freed African slaves and Native Americans encountered one another and shared their treasured wisdoms in the petri dish of oppression. Later in its journey through the Emancipation and Reconstruction period, the body of Conjure grew fatter with practices, as it encountered poor, marginalized, or oppressed ethnic communities in rural and urban areas alike. Here in the so-called "New World," many of the migrated practices remained intact or were able to grow and adapt as they were influenced by the changing economic, social, and government environment and came in contact with other oppressed or marginalized groups, magic workers, and healers. If one were to identify the single event in North American history that infused it with a mass of magical information from another place, it would be the

African slave trade. There are many factors that supported the preservation and continuation of Conjure (and other magical traditions), and one of the most effective was its ability to change its shape without altering its soul.

Conjure as a folk magic practice does not use initiatory ceremonies like some of the other African-influenced or Diasporic traditions. Transmission of lore and practices to "students" or next generations of practitioners usually happens within families or, when necessary, through apprenticeship with hand-selected inheritors. Though Conjure is very African influenced, and its practice more prevalent in the African American community and under other names that may include rootwork and hoodoo, it is also found in white and other families, depending on the community demographics and the social and economic history of the family and individual worker. Additionally, its shape may change from the influence of local Native Americans where it grew and the type of Christian tradition it synchronized with, broadly Protestant or Catholic. The integration of these religious traditions is a part of both its beauty and its power to adapt, adopt, and grow in ways that ensure its survival and speak to the people who will seek the service of its practitioners. These traditions and their association with, and access to, the tribal spirits and divinities that interpenetrate and control all the powers of life, death, love, war, and health (to name a few forces) were held in such high respect, honoring their inherent worth, sacredness, and power, that they were neither destroyed nor forgotten. Rather, they "shape-shifted" the surface appearance of the practices.

By incorporating the names, images, icons, and sacred doctrine (the Holy Bible) of an enforced conversion to the Christian religion, while bridging and retaining the traditional paradigm and philosophy they had heretofore, the practitioner has been allowed a direct, personal, and accessible relationship with the divine creator, its helpful spirits, and their power. How could the African ancestors predict that nearly 150 years after the end of the slave trade, these syncretic traditions would not merely survive, but also grip the attention of many types of people, expanding their presence and power among diverse groups across the United States and beyond.

The traditions that grew out of this approach have continued to this day, migrating beyond the soil of the South where they were born and carrying their seeds through post-Emancipation and reformed America to this day where they are known as rootwork, hoodoo, Conjure, spirit-work, etc. Though this demonstrates the deep wisdom of the African people and the adaptability of the old ways to reshape in a different cultural setting, it was a way to maintain a beloved relationship with the sacred, while supporting survival through forced conversion and the severe and even deadly results of noncompliance. In the end, it gave rise to some of the most diverse, intact, and powerful magical practices in the world. Metaphysical lemonade from colonialist lemons!

All honor to the African ancestors of North America. May their suffering be healed and their spirits exalted to the highest blessings of heaven. Your work lives on. An example of this is the book, which you, the reader, hold in your hands now. Please understand that this document embodies and transmits more than the printed words contained therein. It is a magical horse carrying a spiritual power that is old, potent, and authentic. If its work speaks deeply to your soul, you might wonder what unseen hands introduced you to it and why. It is my hope that by the time you finish reading it, doing some of its works, contemplating its insight, and experiencing the power of the magic it taps, you will *know* that unseen (but felt) hands have always been guiding you towards the resources to attain spiritual sovereignty and receive all the blessings life has to offer. As Mama Starr says, "Can you hear them whispering?" *Old Style Conjure* is simultaneously and at once:

A bridge mediating the living awareness of Conjure as a continued cultural practice.

A time capsule containing age-honored wisdom across generations of change.

A sacred vessel preserving something so special that neither war, forced migration, hanging ropes, or the horrors of the American slave trade could diminish it.

Yet there is another gem of invaluable worth in this document, and that is Starr—her voice and her spirit. This amazing woman and all she does are infused with the very essence of Conjure, and it flows out of her with the natural ease that, for me, is one of the hallmarks of a worker who comes from the soul of the work, and this can only happen by being of the living culture of this practice. Yes, by definition of its form, you are holding a book. Yet, I assure you, it's so much more! It is my pleasure to introduce you to the full face of this container of cherished heirlooms, priceless wisdoms, and more; it is a link into a practice that is thousands of years old with roots so deep that no horror in the human world could diminish its unconquerable spirit. That practice is known as American Southern Conjure. So, here we are at a conjure crossroads: where your presence, Starr's wisdom, my foreword, and your ancestors meet, with something to be revealed.

The subject of *Old Style Conjure* echoes from ancient powers, potent spirits, meaningful magic, and a legacy of wisdom preserved and transmitted through the unbreakable spirit of a people who truly knew its sacred value to the relationship between humanity, divinity, and living ancestry. Starr Casas invites us into a rare treat indeed. With open hands (or pages) the time-tested value, inherent wisdom, and practical applications of a cross-generational living magical tradition are offered. As such, the collective spirit of this book has a true lineage and, with it, a powerful story about its journey to and through America contained in the hearts, bodies, souls, and spirit of its first children, the African slaves who in my humble opinion are the ancestors and angels of American Southern Conjure. The forced journey of these African ancestors from their motherland and the torturous migration across thousands of miles of ocean, then the laborious toils on the plantations of the South, and the intense pressure of life through the cultural vice grip of the Civil War and walking through the life of a family tradition across hundreds of years of time are poured into the book that you hold in your hands. The best way to honor their journey is to build a better life with their wisdom and add yours so that the journey of Conjure continues on to those beyond you.

At the thinning time when shadows move apart.
Sadness fades and frees the haunted heart.
Four roads from everywhere to somewhere meet.
At a crossroads, where spirits and conjure greet;
Four roads from everywhere to somewhere meet,
Let us walk the magic road with practical feet,
    The way is open . . .

—ORION FOXWOOD, Southern Appalachian
conjure worker, faery seer and elder, traditional craft, author of *The Candle and the Crossroads* and *The Flame in the Cauldron*

INTRODUCTION

I HAVE NEVER BEEN a long-winded writer; I prefer to get straight to the point. I want this book to be easy to read, but I also want folks who are new to this work to understand how to do it. In the past, some of my students have told me that I assume everyone knows what I know and that I need to explain things in more detail. So I am gonna write this book a little different from the other fifteen I have written. I am going to try and write in a way even the novice worker will understand, and the information will also maybe help the seasoned worker as well. I feel that it is important for this work to be passed on, as many of the elders are passing and with them the knowledge they hold. I don't want this work to die out; it is too important to my culture.

Conjure is a living culture. Conjure has been passed down from one family member to another. It is a set of remedies, tales, and what folks outside the culture call "spells" but conjure workers simply call "works." Conjure is not dead, nor does it need to be changed or upgraded! Folks tend to think that if works don't have tons of hard-to-find ingredients or a bunch of stuff you need to do, then they will not work; or that they are just a bunch of ole wives' tales, because nothing so simple can be powerful.

Those remedies and wives' tales have been working since they were brought here on the first slave ship by the ancestors.

It is a way of life and ingrained in Southern folks from child-hood. Southern folks have a whole different way of looking at life than folks from other parts of the country. That same culture is ingrained within this work. This knowledge has been passed down from one family member to the next or from an elder—it was not out in the public. This work was never supposed to be out in the world like it is today. The minute it was put out on the internet all of that changed.

Over the last ten years this work has been watered down and whitewashed. It has been weakened by some who feel it is okay to leave out works or to mix and mox the work with other works from other modalities. (Thanks to my friend Aunt Sindy for this word; it's not one I use but it fits here.) This work is powerful in itself, so there is no need to change it; it is a powerhouse on its own. It is my goal to keep the tradition and culture alive with every book I write. Within these pages, I am gonna share information that will help the folks who pick this book up to understand how to do the work.

Southern children are taught from a very early age to respect their elders. In my world that is serious business. My mama used to tell us that if "we didn't respect our elders, then we therefore didn't respect ourselves." I'm in my sixties, and I still say "yes, mam" and "no, mam" or "yes sir, no sir" to folks who are older than me. Respect is an important ingredient in this work also: you have to be respectful of the ancestors and respectful of the spirits you call upon to help you get the job done.

Responsibility is another big one. You are responsible for every work you do. There is no "rule of three" or any other rule to keep you in check; it's totally on your shoulders. Conjure workers are taught that as long as a work is justified, then there will be no harmful effects to the practitioner should their target be smart enough to do a reversal.

As a conjure worker, it is important to remember every action causes a reaction; and it is also important that you never do this work in a fit of anger. There is no fairy godmother sitting on your shoulder to protect you if you do unjustified work on a target. (The target is the person being worked on.)

Don't let the simplicity of this work fool you into thinking that this work is all sugary sweet; it's not. Some works can be dangerous if the worker isn't careful; the work can backfire on the practitioner. Here's a small example—and there will be more throughout the book. Hotfoot work is something done to move someone out quickly where they will not come back. This is not work to be taken lightly; this type of work should only be done when everything else fails. When you work with hotfoot products on someone, you could be sending their spirit to wander and to be restless. The hotfoot work could cause them to never have peace and to just move from place to place.

I have seen more folks have this work backfire on them than I can shake a stick at. Hotfoot work should never be done in anger or for a small offence, such as gossip or just because someone made you mad. There may be a time and place for this type of work, but just because you are upset with someone doesn't make it right. Always remember that work must be justified, you must be responsible for your actions, and you should always remember every action causes a reaction. If a target decided to do a reversal, you could be hit by your own work. Be mindful before you jump into a work with both feet.

I have never been one to beat around the bush and drag out my writings. I like to keep it simple and straight to the point. You don't have to have a chemical degree or be a scholar to be a conjure worker, nor do you have to spend thousands of dollars on supplies. In the time of the ancestors, they weren't allowed to leave the plantation, so they worked with what they had or with what could be found around the home.

As you will find within these pages, you simply have to have a strong faith in yourself and in your God, and you must know the work will be a total success! You also need to have the ingredients.

Here's a little example of how Conjure works. If you need to draw prosperity into your home, then for five days at sunrise, you would write out your need on a piece of paper as the hands of the clock are moving upward towards the hour. Then burn this petition to ash. Once the ash cools, hold it in your hand and step outside. Face the east and call on the Trinity. To call on the Holy Trinity, you simply say, "I call on God the Father, God the Son, and God the Holy Spirit" (or "Holy Ghost," as some folks say). Then you pray your petition. The petition expresses what you need and require. Once you have finished your prayer, you blow the ash to the east. This is a very simple, but effective work.

Please don't think that just because the work seems simple that it isn't powerful or effective. Conjure came from the horrors of slavery. This work has the power of all those who have gone before us, those ancestors of Conjure who suffered untold things that no human should have to suffer. They are the foundation of this work.

There will be more information about how Conjure came to be later on.

Another very important thing that needs to be understood is that the Bible is built into Conjure. It is a large part of this work, even though some folks may wish it wasn't so. There are powerful works in the Bible—if you know where to find them.

In the days of slavery, this work focused on protection, uncrossing, "law stay away," and other works that helped keep the ancestors safe. On the plantation, there was no need for money or prosperity, but when freedom arrived, folks needed money in order to live, so other works were born out of necessity.

Teaching for as long as I have has shown me that a lot of folks who come into Conjure really don't understand the culture that these works come from. When I was growing up, I spent every summer with my grandma and aunties in South Carolina. I eventually moved there and went to school.

My relations worked in the tobacco and cotton fields, as did I. I never had to pick cotton, thank God, but I did work under the tobacco barn and in the field suckering and picking tobacco. Every family had the same routine. Go to work, knock off at noon, and go home until around two in the afternoon, then back to the barn until late afternoon.

This was five days a week and most times a half a day on Saturday. The rest of Saturday was spent in town shopping. That is the only time they went to the grocery store in town. If they needed something during the week, it was bought at one of the little stores around the area. On Sundays you had to go to the prayer house. This was how it was for as long as I can remember.

The reason I am telling about this is to show that there was no time to run to the store and buy supplies for a conjure job. The store in town was about a thirty-minute drive, and most families didn't own a car. The ancestors used what they had at home or in the woods. Old flannel long johns were used to make conjure bags, old clothes were used to make dollies, oil lamps were worked with because that's what they used for light, and brooms were used to sweep things away or draw them in; the list goes on and on. The point is there was no extra money to spend on conjure supplies—every penny counted. Money was tight for everyone that worked in the fields and under the barn unless you lived in the big house.

There is a lot more to Conjure than what most folks think. I hope by the time you finish this book that you will see uses for many of the items you have in your home. You have more conjure tools around you than you know. A lot of the items you have in your pantry can be worked with. As you read these pages, please keep an open mind.

For example, here are a few works that can help with dandruff and also to keep unwanted spirits out of the house.

A good safe treatment to control dandruff and keep your scalp clean from buildup is apple cider vinegar. I use plain vinegar in a spray bottle about every two weeks on my scalp. You can use a mixture of half water and half vinegar. You need a rag to tie your hair up with. Spray the mixture directly on your scalp, make sure you get any of the scalp area where there is itching. Once the scalp is saturated, then you need to tie your head with a rag. Let the mixture stand on the scalp for about twenty minutes, then wash your hair.

Q. What is a crossed condition?

A. A crossed or cross condition can be a long run of bad luck, money problems that just will not go away, or long-term fussing and fighting in the home. A crossed condition can also cause some type of illness the doctors can't find a reason for.

Q. I am having a run of bad luck. Am I jinxed?

A. Everyone has a run of bad luck every once in a while. It doesn't always mean you are jinxed or crossed. You can add the wash below to a tub of water and do a cleansing bath if you feel like there is something else going on. Remember to dress the crown of your head and the bottom of your feet after any type of spiritual bath.

Q. What is a wash?

A. A wash is made with ingredients just like you would make a tea. Sometimes roots, herbs, rocks, and even a pinch of dirt can be added to a mixture.

Q. What does dressing mean?

A. To dress something is to put oil upon it, be it a door, your body, or some other material item.

Vinegar is also good for clearing away jinxes, crossed conditions, and general bad luck. You can make a wash with a half a cup of vinegar, four tablespoons of table salt, and a squeezed lemon. You add all the ingredients to a bucket of water and then you pray Psalm 23 over the bucket. Use a white cloth and wash your doors of your home inside and out with the mixture.

Let the doors air-dry, then you come back with some olive oil that you have prayed Psalm 23 over and dress your doors. Make a cross with the oil on the four corners of the door and one in the center of the door as you pray your petition for safety and protection. This should be done once a month. Use leftover wash to scrub your door stoop and sidewalk with.

Psalm 23 V 1–6

1 The Lord is my shepherd; I shall not want.

2 He maketh me to lie down in green pastures: he leadeth me beside the still waters.

3 He restoreth my soul: he leadeth me in the paths of righteousness for his name's sake.

4 YEA, THOUGH I WALK THROUGH THE VALLEY OF THE SHADOW OF DEATH, I WILL FEAR NO EVIL: FOR THOU ART WITH ME; THY ROD AND THY STAFF THEY COMFORT ME.

5 THOU PREPAREST A TABLE BEFORE ME IN THE PRESENCE OF MINE ENEMIES: THOU ANOINTEST MY HEAD WITH OIL; MY CUP RUNNETH OVER.

6 SURELY GOODNESS AND MERCY SHALL FOLLOW ME ALL THE DAYS OF MY LIFE: AND I WILL DWELL IN THE HOUSE OF THE LORD FOR EVER.

This is a simple but powerful way to cleanse your home. Anytime there is fussing and fighting or things just feel out of sorts, a lil cleansing wash around the home can set things right again.

CONJURE BASICS Q&A

I KNOW SOME FOLKS will have a lot of questions about this work, while others who read the book will already know what I am talking about. I want to go over some general questions here.

Q. What is Conjure?

A. Conjure is magic, plain and simply. Conjure was brought over by the slaves from Africa. It is a combination of culture, beliefs, and knowledge brought over by the ancestors.

Q. Where did Conjure come from?

A. Conjure was brought to North America from Africa with the first slaves.

Q. Is it the same work that was done in the African homeland?

A. No! That was not possible. For one thing, the roots, herbs, trees, and the land in general were different. The ancestors weren't allowed to bring anything with them, so none of the things from their homeland came along with them here. Instead, they found things over here that worked for them. So the answer is no, it is not possible for it to be the same exact work.

Q. *Who are the ancestors of Conjure?*

A. The ancestors of Conjure are the slaves that were captured and brought here on the slave ships to be sold, carrying only their knowledge.

Q. *Were the ancestors of Conjure Christians?*

A. This question has caused many debates and outright battles. Some folks still refuse to accept the fact that Conjure is hidden within Christianity.

Christianity was already in Africa by the time the ancestors were captured. History tells us this. Those who were not Christians when they were captured were soon forced to become Christians, and they made Christianity work for them, as we will see over and over in this book. So to answer the question: yes, the ancestors of Conjure were Christians.

Q. *Can white folks do conjure work?*

A. Yes, they can, as long as they honor the ancestors of this work. Those ancestors are the folks who were kidnapped and sold into slavery. They brought this work here and deserve to be honored. And who better to honor them than white folks who at one time enslaved them?

Q. *What is a two-headed worker?*

A. A two-headed worker is a worker who works with both hands! This means that they can heal or curse, not just one or the other. Most conjure workers are two-headed workers.

Q. *How does the Bible fit into Conjure?*

A. When the ancestors were forced into Christianity, they hid a lot of their works within the Bible, the spirituals they sang, and the stories they told. It is important that it is understood that as slaves they had no freedom! They had no say in the way they worshipped, but they were smart! They hid their worship within Christianity.

Q. Is Conjure a religion?

A. No! Most conjure workers are Christian, but Conjure is not a religion. Conjure is work that brings about change with prayers, the Bible, roots, herbs, and other ingredients.

Q. Do you have to be initiated?

A. No! There is no initiation or priesthood in Conjure.

Q. Is Conjure the same thing as Santeria or Palo?

A. No! It is a set of works that came out of slavery. It is not a religion.

Q. Are the works in Santeria or Palo the same works as in Conjure?

A. No! They are not. They may be similar, but they are not the same. The work is done differently, and the ingredients used are not the same.

Q. Do you have to be a Christian to be a conjure worker?

A. No, you do not have to be a Christian. But if you remove the Bible, then you are no longer doing conjure work; you are doing something else. The Bible is an integral part of Conjure. There are a lot of folks who would love to take the Bible out of Conjure, but if you do, then it is no longer Conjure. You have to separate the Bible from the churches, because the churches are man-made and men make the rules. Why would you throw a powerful book away just because you don't like the church or the folks who run it? This work is very powerful, and it stands alone without a bunch of hocus pocus to make it be effective.

Q. Who are the ancestors?

A. The ancestors are your blood kin that have passed on. Sometimes folks outside the bloodline become ancestors. If you have a mentor or someone you love dearly, they could become your ancestor.

Q. What is an altar?

A. In conjure work, the altar is a place to say your prayers and meet Spirit. A conjure altar can be as simple as a table covered with a cloth, or it can be as elaborate as you want it to be.

Q. What is the Holy Trinity?

A. The Holy Trinity is God the Father, God the Son, and God the Holy Spirit or Holy Ghost; the sacred number three.

Q. What is a conjure hand?

A. A conjure hand can be a packet, a mojo bag, or a jack ball. Each one of them is made a little differently, but they are all still conjure hands.

* A packet is a piece of red flannel cloth that the ingredients have been loaded into, then it is folded onto a square and you stitch it shut.

* A mojo bag is a small red flannel bag that is hand sewn, then the ingredients are loaded into the bag and it is tied shut.

* A jack ball is different from the packet and the conjure bag because it is wrapped with red cotton string until the ingredients are covered in the shape of a ball.

Q. *Is a conjure dollie the same as a voodoo doll?*

A. No! A conjure dollie is usually made to represent a target that will be worked on. This dollie is named for the target and may be loaded with the target's personal concerns such as hair, nail clippings, or maybe a photo. Most of the time, a voodoo doll is made to honor the spirits, but they can also be made to represent a target for a work aimed at a target.

Q. *Is prayer important?*

A. Yes! Prayer is a big part of Conjure.

Q. *Do conjure workers believe in karma?*

A. No! The concept of karma does not exist in Conjure. This doesn't mean that you can just run wild. Conjure workers believe that it's okay to do any type of work as long as it's justified. In that case, there will be no repercussions.

Q. *What does "justified" mean?*

A. In conjure work "justified" basically means that the target has to have done you a wrong. I don't mean a slight or they made you mad; you have to have a good reason for the work. It is really important that you understand that you and you alone are responsible for your actions; so make sure you have a good reason for doing the work. Just because you don't like someone is not a good enough reason.

Q. Do works have to be justified?

A. Yes. As a rule, anytime you work on someone, the work should be justified. The "every action causes a reaction" rule works here. You can't cross someone up just because they pissed you off. That would be unjust. Also, if your target did a reversal, then you would get hit by your own work.

Q. What is a "reversal"?

A. A reversal is a set of works that can be done to turn a situation around. Let's say you have had a run of really bad luck and nothing you have done has changed it. You might need to do a set of reversal works to remove whatever is there, and if someone caused your bad luck, they will get it right back. The only way to do a reversal is to utilize a counterclockwise motion. It's like turning back the hand of the clock—you're reversing what's been done. Here's an example of an easy reversal:

1. First, hold a plain white unlit stick candle in your hand.

2. Starting at the crown of your head, circle your body in a counterclockwise motion, moving downwards. Make sure to circle your head and shoulders.

3. When you reach your torso, rather than circling, brush the candle against yourself in a downward and outward motion.

4. Finally, light the candle and pray that whatever is there be removed and sent back wherever it came from.

Q. What do you need to be a good worker?

A. You need faith in yourself to start with. At least 50 percent of this work is the "knowing" it will be a success, claiming success the minute the need for the work arrives. You cannot second-guess yourself or your work. If you do, then you are wasting your time.

Q. Will I go to hell for doing conjure work?

A. Absolutely not! Conjure work is done in the belief that anything one does as justified work is okay. You can't be blamed for doing work that is justified.

Q. Will I be harmed if I work for folks?

A. Some folks tend to be worried about doing works on behalf of others, so I wanted to face that question here. This is a tricky question, because it really has a yes answer and a no answer.

I'll start with the yes. Yes, you can be harmed if you work on someone and you do not have your protections up and you do not do a cleansing after the work.

No, you can't be harmed as long as you are protected, keep up with your cleansing work, and only do justified works.

Q. Am I doing black magic?

A. No! Conjure workers do not have anything to do with black magic. Conjure workers only do justified works; they do not put magic on folks with the intent to harm.

Q. How do I know if a curse is real or not?

A. The very first thing you need to do is divination to see what is really going on and if you indeed have a curse on you or if you are just having a run of bad luck.

Q. *How do I know if I am being conjured?*

A. Usually when someone has been worked on, signs will manifest. It may just start out as bad luck or your money going out the door, where you end up barely having enough to live on. It could manifest in one accident after the other or everything going wrong at the same time. Family problems just keep happening, one thing after another, or unexplained illnesses just won't go away and when checked out by a doctor they can't find anything wrong. The list can go on and on, but it has to be a continuation of things. One or two things are not enough to claim someone is conjured. The best way to find out for sure is to have a consultation with a worker.

Q. *How do I reverse being conjured?*

A. There are a set of works called cleansings and reversal works. The cleansing works can be done through some kind of spiritual bath or a brush-down with a candle or with a broom. A brush-down with a chicken foot will also cleanse.

To reverse work, there are sets of works that can be done. Here is an easy reversal:

1. Hold a small unlit stick "taper" candle in your hand and circle it around your head three times counterclockwise.

2. Brush yourself with the candle in a downward direction.

3. Light the candle and let it burn out.

4. Repeat this process daily for twenty-one days. It is preferable to do this after sunset, but you could do it at anytime, as long as the minute hand of the clock is going downward. In other words, between one minute after

the hour to twenty-nine minutes after the hour. (When the minute hand moves from the half-hour mark toward the hour—from 7:30 to 8:00, for example—then it is moving upward and it is not the right time for this kind of work.)

PHOTOS BY ARTHUR SEVERIO

Q. Can I start a candle work, then stop the work until the next day? Will it affect the work?

A. I hear this question over and over again from folks who have been told that if they put a candle out during the work it will affect the work and the work will not be a success. This is some rule that someone set for themselves, and it has been passed around and has become some folks' truth. I can't speak for other modalities, but there are no such rules in conjure work.

The truth is that sometimes it is good to let a work rest in between workings. You should put the candles out after you say your prayers. It all depends on the work you are doing. Also, for various reasons, some folks can't leave a candle burning in their home indefinitely and must put it out. This should not affect the work as long as you do the work daily.

Q. Can I blow out a candle?

A. This is a secret I have never before shared. Here is a work to remove someone from your life:

1. First, write the target's name on a stick candle using a knife.

2. Then when the hands of the clock are going down, light the candle, while calling out the target's name three times.

3. Let the candle burn for five minutes. Then call their name three times again and then blow the candle out.

4. Repeat the process daily until the candle is burnt out.

5. Throw any leftover wax in the crossroads.

So you see, sometimes you can blow out a candle!

Q. Can I use matches to light my candles?

A. Yes, you can. Ole folks say that the sulfur from the matches will drive the devil away.

Q. How does the family live with a conjure worker?

A. For me and my family, this has never been an issue. My children grew up around my mama, so it was just natural to them. My mama treated my husband and his mama was a worker, so there has never been an issue. He did tell me once, that if he had known I was like his mama, he would probably not have married me.

I wasn't insulted. I took it as a compliment, because his mama was a very powerful woman. Like my mama, she took care of business. Most workers who are not raised in the culture don't have it that easy. Sometimes they have to even go as far as hiding the work from family members.

My advice is to take it slow. Introduce the work in small doses. Maybe start with a prosperity working or something that they will see as helping and positive. Don't try to shove it in their faces. Take your time and let them get used to the work, little by little. They may never approve and, if that is the case, then just do your work in private.

Conjure is about tricks: you have to learn how to hide your work, while still doing it in plain sight. Just take it real slow; there isn't any rush.

OLE TIME RELIGION

Wrestle On Jacob

I hold my brudder wid a trebling hand,
De Lord will bless my soul,
Wrastl on Ja-cob, Ja-cob day is a breakin.
My sister, Brudder Jacky, All de member
I would not let him go.
Wrastl' on Ja-cob, Oh he would not let him go
2. I will not let you go, my Lord
3. Fisherman Peter was out at sea
4. He cast all night and he cast all day
5. He catch no fish, but he catch some soul
6. Jacob hang from a trembling limb
I looked to the East at the breaking of the day,
The old ship of Zion went sailing away.

SOME OF THE WRITINGS you find in Conjure are different than the English most folks speak. That is because this is the Gullah language, as it is still spoken today by the Gullah people, an African American population living on the Sea Islands and coastal areas of South Carolina, Georgia, and northeastern Florida. Gullah is recognized by the US government as a real language; it is not some distant dialect spoken in the past. This is the living language of the Gullah Nation and still very much alive.

In order to really understand Conjure and the culture it comes from, you have to understand the way the ancestors thought. If you were a Southern child, raised in a home where a worker lived, you would have been taught these secrets as you were growing up.

Most folks, when they look at the spiritual above, see a spiritual that talks about Peter fishing and not catching any fish. They don't understand that the words really have nothing to do with Peter. It's a coded message to let folks know what is going on. The prayer house or meetinghouse was the only place the ancestors were allowed to meet and worship. They learned to sing spirituals that the slave masters thought were just church songs, but some were sharing information like the one above.

So what is the message above? You just have to know what you are looking for.

In this spiritual "I hold my brudder wid a trebling hand" lets us know they are afraid. "Wrastl on Ja-cob, Ja-cob day is a breakin" lets us know that the sun is just rising. "Fisherman Peter was out at sea" lets folks know the plantation owner is out of the house. "He cast all night and he cast all day" says he's been out searching all day and all night. "He catch no fish, but he catch some soul" means he caught the ancestor he was looking for, and—"Jacob hang from a trembling limb"—he hung him. "I looked to the East at the breaking of the day, the old ship of Zion went sailing away" tells folks they hung him the next day at daybreak. The old ship Zion is his spirit leaving him, going up into the East to heaven, where it is said the dead will rise on Judgment Day.

As you can see this spiritual really isn't all about biblical matters. It's to let the slaves on the plantation know what was going on. This song really has nothing to do with the biblical Jacob or Peter, but it has *everything* to do with a runaway slave that got caught and was hung at daybreak the next day.

You may be thinking, *What in the world does this ole spiritual have to do with learning Conjure!?* My answer is everything. It will teach you to really look at everything.

Conjure workers are tricky and cunning: they are taught to drop work in plain sight, to bless or curse right in front of a target without the target being any the wiser. Just like in this ole spiritual, a message hidden in plain view. Folks who were not raised in this culture are missing that advantage.

I wanted to start with a spiritual to give y'all an idea of how the ancestors thought. You have to forget about modern times and all the conveniences we have today. Some will know what I am talking about. Younger folks may be shocked at how little folks had in the days of the ancestors, especially compared to what we have today.

Conjure is not modern. It was born out of a time when one person was allowed to own another, a time when folks' lives depended on hiding information, a time when a person could be killed or maimed for something as simple as spilling a cup of water. It's ugly, it's horrible, and it is beyond belief—but it is the truth and it is from this place that this work was born. The work is mingled in everything we do in our daily lives. This work is not something you just *do*. It becomes a way of life.

I want to examine one more spiritual. This one is called "Go in the Wilderness," and this spiritual, like the previous one, is a coded message:

Go in the Wilderness

Jesus call you. Go in de wilderness,
Go in de wilderness, go in de wilderness,
Jesus call you. Go in de wilderness
To wait upon de Lord.
Go wait upon do Lord,

Go wait upon de Lord,
Go wait upon de Lord, my God,
He take away de sins of de world.
Jesus a-waitin'. Go in de wilderness,
Go, &c.
All dem chil'en go in de wilderness
To wait upon de Lord

If you are truly going to understand Conjure and the culture it comes from, then first you must understand the ancestors. You have to really look at slavery with opened eyes, not with blinders on. Everything they did was watched twenty-four hours a day, seven days a week. They worked from sunup till sundown.

My mama worked like this, when she was a child. All of my aunts did, too, to help my grandma feed them. They went to school when they could. They lived in a house supplied by the man my grandma worked for. She was nothing more than a field hand, as were her children. My granddaddy was crippled and couldn't work.

As we know, the ancestors learned to pass messages along in song. They would sing while they worked in the fields. Look at "Go in the Wilderness": it is a message of where to go and what to do.

So "Jesus" called: this is telling them that word has come and the time to move is now. The next stanza tells them to go into the "wilderness," which of course means the woods. They are to go there and wait. "He take away de sins of de world" is telling them that the contact will take them away from the plantation. The "Lord" is waiting for them, which means the contact is there.

The plantation owner didn't have a clue as to what was going on, until it was too late. The ancestors had to think fast on their feet to stay alive; that same cleverness is in the work. Conjure workers are very tricky when it comes to the work of laying down tricks. Go and listen to some of the ole spirituals. Find what is hidden there, it will help you in your work. Throughout the book I will share more unseen wisdoms.

Now let's talk about the prayer house and religion. The topic of religion is a heated topic among some who claim this work sometimes, but the facts cannot be denied. Most conjure workers are Christian. The slaves that were kidnapped were forced to become Christian, at least by the third generation if not before.

Folks will argue that the ancestors who were brought over here weren't Christians; I don't disagree with that even though Christianity existed in Africa at the time of slavery. I am by no means trying to turn this into a history lesson, but I do think that this is important to readers who are just coming into this work.

I understand that Christianity was forced on most of the ancestors and that most likely it was not their religion when they were captured. However, having been raised in this culture, I also know for a *fact* that until fifteen or twenty years ago almost everyone in the rural South was Christian; most elders still are.

The folks of the Gullah Nation, descendants of the first slaves who landed on the shores, still speak their own language and are Christians, although they practice their own form of Christianity. They worship as their ancestors did. You don't have to take my word for this: the Gullah are alive and well in the Low Country and islands of Georgia and South Carolina. Go see for yourself.

It's confusing nowadays: you got one set of folks saying that the ancestors were not Christians, another set saying there is no Christianity in the work, then folks like me who were raised in the culture and who were raised to believe and taught that the Old Testament is a large part of this work. I understand that folks want it to be as it was in Africa, but that is not being realistic. And if I am anything, it is realistic. There is no way the ancestors were allowed to worship as they did in Africa; they weren't even allowed to hold meetings of any kind. They couldn't gather together to visit, much less worship. I grew up on these stories; to not believe them would be calling my mama and my elders liars, and that will never happen!

There came a time when the slaves were forced to become Christian. Let me tell you that the ancestors were a lot smarter than they were given credit for. This trait is still alive today in a lot of rural Southern families. When we were young children, my mama taught us to let folks see what they want to see; don't try to convince them any differently. This is exactly what the ancestors did. The plantation owners wanted Christians, and so they got Christians.

The prayer house was the only place the ancestors were allowed to gather in a group. They weren't allowed to have drums or other instruments that they worshipped with in their homeland nor could they worship in their own way. The slave owners did this to keep down revolts. The plantation owners were afraid of the drum and the way the ancestors worshipped. They were forced to worship the way the master did. They had no rights or freedoms. This didn't stop them though! Even under such oppression, they still found a way to worship their own way. It is important to note that not all of the ancestors came from the same place. They came from different tribes and nations in many parts of Africa with different beliefs, but they shared a common enemy: the slaver and the slave owner.

You had the field hands, who were tormented and abused by the white overseers, and the house help, which were treated a little better, but they overcame the issues they faced daily to come together for the greater good. Being free to worship varied from plantation to plantation. On some plantations, the freedom to worship was forbidden, and if caught, the offenders would be punished.

These ancestors were smart and cunning; they Africanized Christianity to suit them. (Thank you, Robert Lucas, for putting the word "Africanized" out there! Robert is a wonderful reader and worker; he can be found at *www.ancestorhealing.org*.) What exactly does this mean? They incorporated African-style dance and singing, along with the Bible and the hymns to make their own way of worship. They couldn't have drums so instead they invented the foot stomp, and of course, there was a lot of hand clapping. All of these things still live on with the Gullah Nation.

The ancestors worshipped different from the white folks. They danced with the spirits and made their own religion. The ring shout is a good example of how they danced with Spirit. The ring shout is a way of calling down Spirit. The ring shout consists of going around in a circle slowly, while shuffling and stomping your feet, clapping your hands, and singing. No shouting is involved. This is a good way to get Spirit moving.

The prayer house became a place where the ancestors could find peace in prayer and share Spirit with others. These folks had to work from sunup till sundown, yet they still went to the prayer house for worship. They made Christianity their own. They worshipped and uplifted their spirits with a mixture of

Christianity and the faith from their homeland. This way of worship still exists today.

Conjure workers are a different kind of Christian than the mainstream Christian. Conjure workers, like the ancestors, are more spirit-led in their beliefs. Have you ever seen an elder in church swaying and waving a handkerchief over their head? Did you know that practice also came from the ancestors? Swaying is to draw down the spirit and the waving of the white handkerchief is an offering to Spirit. So much information is being lost.

Another difference between a Christian conjure worker and a more mainstream Christian is that conjure workers don't see everything in black and white; there is always that gray area where justice is served. It's not a "sin" or against God's will if the work is justified. So, if there is an issue that needs to be resolved and it is a justified issue, it's ok to go to church and scream for justice. Just remember, as the ole folks say, "Our time ain't God's time." So He might take a minute to answer your prayer.

WORKS FROM THE BIBLE

I want to share a few works from the Bible with you. The first one is for deliverance from an enemy.

Deliverance from an Enemy

Take a white candle and brush yourself off with it starting at the crown of your head to the bottom of your feet while praying for deliverance. Light the candle and pray Nehemiah 9 V 27–28 over the candle. Pray over the candle daily until it burns out.

NEHEMIAH 9 V 27–28

27 THEREFORE THOU DELIVEREDST THEM INTO THE HAND OF THEIR ENEMIES, WHO VEXED THEM: AND IN THE TIME

OF THEIR TROUBLE, WHEN THEY CRIED UNTO THEE, THOU
HEARDEST THEM FROM HEAVEN; AND ACCORDING TO THY
MANIFOLD MERCIES THOU GAVEST THEM SAVIOURS, WHO
SAVED THEM OUT OF THE HAND OF THEIR ENEMIES.

28 BUT AFTER THEY HAD REST, THEY DID EVIL AGAIN
BEFORE THEE: THEREFORE LEFTEST THOU THEM IN THE
LAND OF THEIR ENEMIES, SO THAT THEY HAD THE DOMIN-
ION OVER THEM: YET WHEN THEY RETURNED, AND CRIED
UNTO THEE, THOU HEARDEST THEM FROM HEAVEN; AND
MANY TIMES DIDST THOU DELIVER THEM ACCORDING TO
THY MERCIES.

Justice Against an Enemy

Light a red candle and pray 2 Samuel 22 V 49–51 and your
petition. This work is meant to bring forth justice.

2 SAMUEL 22 V 49–51

49 AND THAT BRINGETH ME FORTH FROM MINE ENEMIES:
THOU ALSO HAST LIFTED ME UP ON HIGH ABOVE THEM THAT
ROSE UP AGAINST ME: THOU HAST DELIVERED ME FROM THE
VIOLENT MAN.

50 THEREFORE I WILL GIVE THANKS UNTO THEE, O LORD,
AMONG THE HEATHEN, AND I WILL SING PRAISES UNTO THY
NAME.

51 HE IS THE TOWER OF SALVATION FOR HIS KING: AND
SHEWETH MERCY TO HIS ANOINTED, UNTO DAVID, AND TO
HIS SEED FOR EVERMORE.

The ancestors used the Bible to their advantage; the Bible
holds many hidden works. They showed the slave master what
he wanted to see, which is how conjures are taught to do. Let

folks see what they want to see; it's all a trick. Folks will believe whatever they want. This works to the workers' advantage, just like it worked for the ancestors. The ancestors had to be seen without really being seen. This is one of the greatest lessons you can learn.

Don't let your ego get the best of you; do your work and let folks see whatever they choose to see. It really has nothing to do with you; your goal should always be the work. The knowledge of the work is the power you need to have success in your life. Learn to see what is hidden and work with it towards making your life better. Listen closely and keep your eyes open. Listen for what's not being said and what is unseen!

No one can teach you how to pray, that is something that you have to learn on your own. The best way to start is to just start talking asking God for his blessings and to remove all blocks out of your way. Some of those I have helped have told me that they felt foolish at first and were uncomfortable talking to air, but the more they have prayed, the better they feel about doing it.

I picked up praying as a young child in church. I can't even imagine what it would be like to be an adult and not know how to pray for the blessings I needed to have brought into my life. Prayer really is nothing more than pouring your heart out to Spirit and asking for the help you need in your life. There is no hocus pocus to it. Words hold power, and Spirit listens to the words we speak. Don't make praying harder than it is; just open your heart and let the words flow. That's all you have to do.

You don't have to kneel, dance around, shout, or anything else. Just start talking to God. The best prayers in the world come from the heart. If you need to pay a bill, but you don't have the money, then pray that money into your hands. You could pray something like this:

"Lord, I am desperate in my need, I need to pay _____. Lord, you said knock and the door shall open! Well Lord, I'm knocking on the door and I need your blessing, so I can pay _____. These are your words, Lord, and as your child I believe that you will provide for me and the doors will be opened for me to pay my _____. The Lord is my Shepherd and I shall not want! Blessed Lord, as you have spoken, so shall it come to light! Dear heavenly Father, I thank you for the blessing to be able to pay _____. In the name of God the Father, God the Son, and God the Holy Ghost. Amen"

Do you see how easy that is? Just lay what is on your heart at God's feet, and he will listen and answer your prayers. Don't worry about how it looks. Just be yourself and pour your heart out. Your miracle is waiting!

The Bible is full of scriptures that can help you in your time of need if you can't find the right words to ask for help. I know some folks are not into reading the Bible, but it really is full of power and can help you achieve your goals. I'm going to share some prayers, chapter and verse, from the Bible to help you.

Here are a few to get you started. There will be more throughout the book.

Prayers Against Enemies

ISAIAH 54 V 17

17 No WEAPON THAT IS FORMED AGAINST THEE SHALL PROSPER; AND EVERY TONGUE THAT SHALL RISE AGAINST THEE IN JUDGMENT THOU SHALT CONDEMN. THIS IS THE HERITAGE OF THE SERVANTS OF THE LORD, AND THEIR RIGHTEOUSNESS IS OF ME, SAITH THE LORD.

LUKE 1 V 74

74 THAT HE WOULD GRANT UNTO US, THAT WE BEING DELIVERED OUT OF THE HAND OF OUR ENEMIES MIGHT SERVE HIM WITHOUT FEAR.

PSALM 27 V 5–6

5 FOR IN THE TIME OF TROUBLE HE SHALL HIDE ME IN HIS PAVILION: IN THE SECRET OF HIS TABERNACLE SHALL HE HIDE ME; HE SHALL SET ME UP UPON A ROCK.

6 AND NOW SHALL MINE HEAD BE LIFTED UP ABOVE MINE ENEMIES ROUND ABOUT ME: THEREFORE WILL I OFFER IN HIS TABERNACLE SACRIFICES OF JOY; I WILL SING PRAISES UNTO THE LORD.

JEREMIAH 39 V 17–18

17 BUT I WILL DELIVER THEE, IN THAT DAY, SAITH THE LORD: AND THOU SHALT NOT BE GIVEN INTO THE HAND OF THE MEN OF WHOM THOU ART AFRAID.

18 FOR I WILL SURELY DELIVER THEE, AND THOU SHALT NOT FALL BY THE SWORD, BUT THY LIFE SHALL BE FOR A PREY UNTO THEE: BECAUSE THOU HAST PUT THY TRUST IN ME, SAITH THE LORD.

2 KINGS 17 V 39

39 BUT THE LORD YOUR GOD YE SHALL FEAR; AND HE SHALL DELIVER YOU OUT OF THE HAND OF ALL YOUR ENEMIES.

ISAIAH 41 V 11–12

11 BEHOLD, ALL THEY THAT WERE INCENSED AGAINST THEE SHALL BE ASHAMED AND CONFOUNDED: THEY SHALL BE AS NOTHING; AND THEY THAT STRIVE WITH THEE SHALL PERISH.

12 THOU SHALT SEEK THEM, AND SHALT NOT FIND THEM, EVEN THEM THAT CONTENDED WITH THEE: THEY THAT WAR AGAINST THEE SHALL BE AS NOTHING, AND AS A THING OF NOUGHT.

PROVERBS 3 V 25–26

25 BE NOT AFRAID OF SUDDEN FEAR, NEITHER OF THE DESO-LATION OF THE WICKED, WHEN IT COMETH.

26 FOR THE LORD SHALL BE THY CONFIDENCE, AND SHALL KEEP THY FOOT FROM BEING TAKEN.

LUKE 1 V 71

71 THAT WE SHOULD BE SAVED FROM OUR ENEMIES, AND FROM THE HAND OF ALL THAT HATE US.

ACTS 18 V 10

10 FOR I AM WITH THEE, AND NO OTHER MAN SHALL SET ON THEE TO HURT THEE: FOR I HAVE MUCH PEOPLE IN THIS CITY.

HEBREWS 13 V 6

6 SO THAT WE MAY BOLDLY SAY, THE LORD IS MY HELPER, AND I WILL NOT FEAR WHAT MAN SHALL DO UNTO ME.

THE FOUNDATION
OF CONJURE

DESPITE ALL THE INFORMATION out there on Conjure, no one to my knowledge has ever written about its foundation. You see plenty of works, or "spells" as outsiders call the work, but there is no mention of the foundation of this work. Is it because folks don't think it's important? Is it because they really don't know? Or is it something else? It really is food for thought. It is one of the first lessons I learned as a young worker and one of the most important.

I have found in today's conjure world that it isn't enough for folks to know the work; they want to "own" the knowledge. They seem to want to claim it when it isn't theirs to claim. This work is borrowed, because it belongs to someone else. Are you wondering what I am talking about? Like my elder Mr. Robert used to say, "Let me break it down for you."

Are you thinking that the foundation of the work is the ingredients that go into the work? If so, you're wrong. The foundation of this work is the ancestors who brought the work over on the slave ships! Conjure didn't exist over here until the slaves were transported here. That's one of the reasons Conjure is part of the South. The ships docked in the South, and all the Southern states were "slave" states! The ancestors' beliefs became part of the Southern culture.

The only thing the kidnapped ancestors had was their knowledge. They didn't have a backpack filled with roots, herbs, and remedies; all that information was in their heads. They only had the clothes that were on their backs. They suffered untold miseries in the bottom of slave ships being taken halfway around the world to an unknown place. Then they were off the ship and on the slave block being sold like animals, but they still had their knowledge and their pride. Can you imagine how much willpower it took to stand docile while in chains and having folks poke and prod you? Or how about never being able to lift your head in pride or to be able to look a white person in the face?

This work—Conjure—came out of their misery and suffering; it came from their blood being spilled. It came from their deaths. The work was done and passed on to help protect the family. The law stay away work was done to keep the slave patrols from finding the runaways. Dollies were made to bind or influence the slave master or overseer. Justice work was done to try and bring justice to an unjust situation. These works came alive from the need to survive.

The blood, suffering, and deaths of the ancestors ensure that this work belongs to them. They should be honored and remembered for their great gift. They are truly the foundation of Conjure, and we must all remember without them there would be no Conjure, Hoodoo, or Rootwork, or whatever name you wish to call the work.

Honoring the ancestors of this work will empower your work. I know this topic makes folks uncomfortable, but it must be discussed in order to give the ancestors their due, which is so sorely lacking. Some folks might not like what I am saying, but that is not my problem. It is theirs.

The ancestors of this work deserve to be honored and uplifted for all that they gave. With more folks getting DNA testing done and finding out family histories, questions can arise. Here are some questions that I have been asked over the years by some of my students.

Q. Do you have to be of African descent to practice Conjure?

A. No, but you must honor and acknowledge the ancestors of this work.

Q. I did an ancestry search and I found out generations back my folks were slavers; can I still be a conjure worker?

A. Yes. What better way to right a wrong than to uplift and honor the ancestors of this work?

Q. My family is racist; do I have the right to do conjure work?

A. Respect and honor go hand in hand. We are not responsible for what others do. We are only responsible for our own actions. If something within you is calling you to this work, then I would say as long as you uplift the ancestors of this work and honor them, then there is no reason why you can't.

Q. What do you mean when you say to honor and uplift the ancestors of Conjure?

A. We are all guests in this work; it doesn't belong to any of us. When I say "honor," I mean for you to maintain a small space for these ancestors, a place where you can offer a cool drink or say a prayer for them. By doing this you are not only showing them respect, but you are feeding their spirits and uplifting them.

I have been asked these four questions many times by new students. The important thing is to understand that we don't have the right to just take this work without giving the ancestors their due. Set up a small altar and dedicate it to the ancestors of Conjure. I have a large altar in my home and the whole family burns lights on it when the need arises, but I am the keeper of the altar. See the photo below.

There are many layers to my ancestor altar; we'll talk more about it in the next chapter. My blood kin and the ancestors of Conjure share the same altar.

To set up the altar, you need a small area. The ideal place is facing the east where the sun rises, but you can really place the altar where you have space. You need a handkerchief to put down on top of the altar space. Place a cool glass of water, a candle, and a Bible on the altar. You can offer the ancestors prayers daily or once a week; it is up to you. I do general altar work every Monday, but you can decide how you want to tend to your altar.

Some folks have a hard time with praying or they just don't know how to pray; that is not an issue. If you are one of those folks, don't get stressed and worried about it. The solution is simple. When you are at your altar, just pick up the Bible and open it up, pray the first passage your eyes fall on. This is called bibliomancy; it is also a good way to do divination. I'll touch more on this later in the book. The point is that you don't have to know how to pray or anything else in order to honor the ancestors.

There may come a time when you want to offer the ancestors more than a candle or prayers. It is important to give them offerings that they like, so you need to know a little about the food they ate. They were given the scraps from the hogs that were butchered, chicken, and the parts of the cow the master didn't want. Somehow they made these foods taste delicious. Some of things that make good offerings are corn bread, greens, fried chicken, boiled peanuts, grits, or smoke, such as cigarettes, cigar, or incense.

I have a set of plates that belong to my mama that I use to place my offerings on, but you can use whatever you have. For those who don't know how to give an offer, I am gonna explain how I give my offerings. This isn't written in stone and you can give your offerings however you want to, as it is very personal. This information is just to help. There will also be more about offerings later.

When I give a food offering, I usually cook whatever I am offering for my family too. I grew up on this food, so for me it's wonderful and makes a good home-cooked meal. I serve the ancestors first—meaning I fix a plate for them. I arrange the food on the plate so the center of the plate is empty for the candle I place there when I offer the plate to them.

I first say my prayers. Then I make a space on my altar for the plate, and then I either use my feet, prayer stick, or clap my hands to call them. I stomp my foot three times, clap three times, or tap the prayer stick on the floor three times. The number three is very powerful as we will see as the book goes on. Hold the plate out slightly over the altar, and with each tap call on the ancestors. Then set the plate on the altar and place the candle in the center of the plate.

Speak with the ancestors and tell them you are giving them an offering, then light your candle. Say some prayers for them or just read a passage out of the Bible for them. You don't have to do a bunch of hocus pocus; just be yourself and let them see that your heart is true. You can leave the offering on the altar for twenty-four hours or for three days. If the candle hasn't burned out by that time, I remove the offering. I take the candle off the plate and place it on the altar so they can still have their light. Then I remove the plate.

Now that you have removed the offering from the altar, what in the world do you do with the remains? Never throw it in the trash; that would be very disrespectful. I dispose of my offering a couple of different ways. It really all depends on the offering and why it is being given. We will cover this in more detail in the offering section of this book. What we have discussed here is a general offering so that you and the ancestors can build a bond. In this case, place the remains of the offering in a brown paper bag. What will you do with this? You can either place the offering at the foot of an oak tree, take it to a park, or bring it to a crossroads. Gently empty the contents of the bag onto the ground, then throw the bag away.

There is no right or wrong way to give an offering. The most important thing is that it is done with honor and respect. Once you build a strong relationship with the ancestors of Conjure, you will see a big difference in how your work turns out. If you want to have a strong foundation in this work, then this relationship with the ancestors is the first step to becoming a great conjurer.

THE ALTAR

WHAT IS AN ALTAR? The altar is nothing more than a home for Spirit to sit. It's the place between places where this world meets the spirit world. It is a place where you can serve Spirit. You can set up an altar in honor of the spirits you work with; the only issue is that if you try to combine with multiple spirits or saints, you must make sure that they will work well together and be at peace with one another.

During slavery times, the ancestors were not allowed to have altars, even within the prayer houses. Their altars consisted of wherever they were doing the work at that moment. Altars are more a product of modern times; my mama didn't have an altar. The kitchen table was where she was always at. The kitchen is the heart of the home, and in the times of slavery, as today, it is where the fire was kept burning.

The truth is the altar can be anywhere or anything. You can leave it up, or you can take it down when you are not serving the spirits that walk with you. It is really up to you. So you can have no altar at all, or you can make it as simple or elaborate as you want it to be. Most folks need to feel connected to Spirit, and the altar will become that connection. The altar is not only a good place to honor Spirit, but it is also a good place for the worker to pray and to petition Spirit.

There is really not a set rule for having an altar space. The first step to having an altar in your home is to figure out where you want the altar to sit; again there is no set place to have the altar. Still, I would like to give you a little direction. I have my ancestor altar facing the east, because that is the place of sunrise and the Bible tells us that the dead will be raised in the east. The east is also the best place for works that are intended to draw things towards you, such as love or money. The sun sets in the west, so the west is the best place for work that is intended to remove, such as banishing. You don't want the spirits you honor to be removed. You want them drawn in to sit on the altar that will become their home over time.

One of my elders, Mimi, told me once that the north is where frost sets and the south is where fire rests. I've always worked with the directions in that way: to cool hotheads they are placed in the north. Cold hearts are placed in the south to heat them up and warm them. The main directions I work with are the east and the west for drawing and removing.

So, you decide where you want to set up your altar with these pieces of information in mind, and then it's time to cleanse the area where the altar will sit.

Make a wash by steeping bay leaves, olive leaves, and three tablespoons of salt together. Make the wash just like you would a cup of tea. Pray Ezekiel 34 V 27 over the wash three times while the wash is cooling.

Ezekiel 34 V 27

27 Then the trees of the field shall yield their fruit, and the earth shall yield her increase. They shall be safe in their land; and they shall know that I am the Lord, when I have broken the bands of their yoke and delivered them from the hand of those who enslaved them.

Once the wash is cooled, strain off the herbs and set them aside. Mix the wash with a little cool water, then clean the area where the altar will sit with the wash. Wipe off the table or whatever the altar will sit on. The floor can also be the altar if you choose to make it so. The important thing is that you are praying and petitioning Spirit as you are working.

After you get your space cleaned and it is dry, you need some type of cloth to cover the space—or to set on the floor if you decided to place the altar on the floor. Some folks will simply use white as an altar cloth, but I have the purple shroud that was on my sister's coffin as the altar cloth on my ancestor altar. The altar is a very personal place; there are no rules to follow when setting up an altar for conjure work. I am going to give you a small list of colors here that may help you decide on a color of cloth to add to your altar.

* Red represents blood, heat, fire, love, and all of these emotions that we feel for folks we love.
* Yellow represents the sun, success, warmth, and happiness.
* Blue represents peace, water, prosperity, and, once again, warmth.
* Green represents growth, money, fertile fields, and life.
* Purple represents power, glory, success, royalty, and mastery.
* White represents purity, power, and faith.
* Black absorbs and holds things; this is a good color for a healing or cleansing altar space.

This is just a little shared information; nothing is written in stone. Follow the spirits that walk with you and decide what color cloth your altar will have.

The next step is to decide what you will have on your altar. There are no hard and fast rules about what items are placed on a conjure altar, but there are a few basic things.

A cool glass of water is needed on the altar to give Spirit a drink; you can also add a cup of coffee as an offering. You need to offer some kind of smoke for them. When I smoked, I gave them a cigarette as an offering. I still do sometimes, but now I like to offer them burning herbs. They seem to like the smoke from the herbs; you can also read the smoke as it whiffs up off the fire. The ancestors will need a candle or an oil lamp. You also need to keep a Bible on the altar, as it helps when you have questions and need answers. This type of Bible work is called bibliomancy.

Bibliomancy is nothing more than divining with the Bible. Hold the Bible in both hands and draw it close to your mouth. Ask your question by kind of pushing your breath out as you speak so your breath flows over the Bible. Then you open the Bible up and read the first passage your eyes fall on; usually you will have your answer. This is a simple but powerful way to get guidance when you are lost and don't know what to do next. You can also find powerful works in the Bible through bibliomancy. The Bible is a strong tool, if you know how to work with it.

Anything else you add to your altar is a bonus. Nowadays money is a big issue with almost everyone, with careers not pay-ing as well as they have in the past, unemployment high, and success seeming just out of reach. In reality, success is never out of reach unless *we* claim it is. Words are power, and if you say some-thing enough, Spirit is going to begin to believe it. So remember whatever you claim is what your spirit will draw to you and into your life. Here is a simple but powerful way to draw prosperity, money, and success into your life. This is called a success altar.

Success Altar

Clean your area and the altar. Your prayer and petition while you are cleaning is "May all blocks and crossed conditions be removed; may only prosperity and success sit here!" I truly believe success and prosperity are a mindset. I want to share a story with you before we move forward to the success altar.

Last week I was going to get a drink at my favorite drive-through, and I passed by an ole business that has been closed for years. Behind the building I saw a tent, and I thought, *dear Lord, someone is homeless living in a tent.* This stayed on my mind. The other day I passed by there again, and a guy was laid back in a chair under the tree with his shades on looking at his phone like he didn't have a care in the world. That is the feel that his spirit was putting off as I looked at him. When I told my granddaughter what I had seen, she laughed and said, "Well Mawmaw, ain't that what you teach us? To act successful and rich even if we only got two cents to our name; any other way of thinking would make us have even less!"

I'm not sure how I like my own teachings given back to me, but she did have a point. Even though he was living in a tent, he didn't have to act like it. He didn't have to claim it. It reminded me of my mama. I wanted a pair of boots one time, and of course, I couldn't get them yet so I said something. I don't even remember what it was, but I remember what she said to me about complaining: "The little girl complained about not having any shoes until she saw the lil boy with no feet!" I will never forget that lil lesson as long as I live.

The points of these stories have everything to do with conjure work and success because we become what we claim we are. At one time, many years ago I wanted to become a writer that would be able to help folks learn through my writings. Here I am writing book after book that just flow out of me. The time has come to stop complaining about what you don't have and start building on what you do have!

Now, let's get that success altar built! We are going to call it the "Crown of Success" altar. Don't go spending a lot of money either; you need to look around your home for the things to add to this altar.

Add a bright cloth to the altar; something that makes you feel good when you look at it or touch the material. Find things to place on your altar that represent success, money, prosperity, and the ideal job or home. This is the tricky part 'cause when we don't have something or it seems out of our reach, we tend to be naysayers. You have to look beyond what is missing to what will fill that void. If you are struggling to finish school, find things that represent graduation and the job you want. If you need a new car, place photos of the one you want on your altar to claim it as yours. Whatever it is that you need or want in your life, place something that represents having it on your altar. Build your dream and make it happen!

After you get your altar built, once a week light a candle, and give a fresh glass of water and any other offering you want to give. We will go into more about the offerings you can share in the next chapter. Give thanks for all you have and all that you will have. Claim the things you want and need in your life. Pull in the success by doing the work and by claiming what is yours. The only person that can stop you is you! Keep them altars going hot.

OFFERINGS

AN OFFERING CAN BE as simple or as elaborate as you want it to be. An offering can be a stone you found somewhere and felt drawn to bring home, or maybe a bird's nest that had fallen out of a tree, or just a simple glass of cool water. It doesn't really matter what is given, but let's be honest with ourselves for a minute: no one works for free. We all expect something for our labor, and Spirit is no different. You wouldn't do a job that you never got paid for. So why in the world should we expect Spirit to work for us without pay?

Spirit will work for you even if you don't leave them an offering, but will work much harder for you when you show your appreciation for their help. By leaving them an offering, not only are you paying them, you are also showing them honor, respect, and love. Spirit loves us enough to come when we call for help. Shouldn't we in turn love them enough to honor them with a gift?

When you go to your job, you work hard, because at the end of the week you know you will get your paycheck. Then why would we think Spirit doesn't want to be paid at the end of a job? I always promise my spirits an offering when the job is done. Like us, they want their pay; therefore they work harder to reach the goal. In my younger years, I would pay Spirit when the job was done, but somewhere over the years, I began to feel like I was bartering with them. I felt like I was saying I don't trust you enough to do the job for me, so I am holding your offering until you follow through with the work. Over time it really became an issue within my own spirit. I began to feel like I was disrespecting my ancestors and the spirits that walk with me.

So I changed the way I had always done it and had been taught to give offerings; I now give them their offerings when I petition them for help. It has been my experience that this way of doing the offerings has made a big difference. You can offer anything you want. They will accept it graciously because you gave the gift with love and appreciation. You can't go wrong. Offerings can be anything you want to give them. I have spirits that are very personal to me, and I always give them things I feel they want. I gave Momi, the Queen of the Waters, an expensive perfume because I felt drawn to do so; she loves good smells. I gave it to her with love, not asking for anything, and she gave me a gift I never thought possible.

The point is that no matter how much the offering costs or doesn't cost, as long as it is given with love and honor, you can't go wrong. I have given rocks that I have found in different places, dollies, bottles, coins, and statues—it just really all depends on you and what you are drawn to give. I will say this: if you are petitioning for something big and you can give a good offering, then it is best to do so. Anything can be given as an offering at the start of the job.

I do want to touch on this important tidbit: Spirit has their own time frame for working; your time isn't always their time. Don't give up, just keep on pushing until your petition is answered.

To call Spirit, you need to tap three times on your altar, and call the spirit's name on each tap. Hold the offering up high; speak in a clear, firm voice and say something like, "I give you this offering with a kind, loving heart." You give the offering with love, honor, appreciation, and respect. Make sure to thank the spirit for all the help they have given you even if you haven't gotten what you are petitioning for yet. You are claiming the petition as a success and in turn telling Spirit that it's a done deal.

Talk to them for a little while. This is the way you build a bond with them. The more you go to them for help, the easier it will become to reach them. Eventually all you will have to do is call on them, and they will come. Leave the offering on your altar for a few days—no longer than a week—and then dispose of it.

You need to make sure you keep a clean glass of water on your altar for them at all times. Once a week light a small tealight in their honor to show that you care about them even when they are not helping you. If you do these small things, you will have success in all your work. They will be happy to come to you.

Anything you feel drawn to offer can be offered. Flowers, whiskey, cigars, stones, money, prayers—whatever you can offer. If I pay with whiskey, I leave it there until it is gone— until it has evaporated. Unless I feel I need to do something else with them, I always leave any stones or money I may have offered on the altar permanently; they belong to Spirit. If the money I leave as offerings builds up, I usually give it to some-one who needs it. I have given up to $300 away out of my money can to someone who needed it. Below is a photo of one of my money cans. I have always been blessed in return. The one thing you cannot do is become greedy; if you do, then you will find yourself spending more and saving less.

Try these little tips the next time you need assistance, and I think you will see a big difference in the outcome of your work.

I have had folks tell me that they push forth their personal power into their work. Well, in the end no matter how much of your personal power you push into your work, you will never be as powerful as Spirit. Sometimes we humans get too full of ourselves and make things harder than they should be. We feel a little power and let our egos get the best of us. This work has no place for overinflated egos, Spirit has a way of letting the air out of those egos if we go too far. In some things, the easy way out is not always the best way, but when you let Spirit do the work for you, it is the road of least resistance. So then why not work and bond with them? It will make everything go with greater speed and success is assured.

Don't overthink this work; every detail does not have to be perfect. Conjure uses what we have on hand in our homes, yards, or the woods around us. Just have faith that your work will be a success and it will be!

DIVINATION

WHAT IS DIVINATION? DIVINATION is a way of finding out what is going on or will go on by spiritual means such as soothsaying and prophecy. Divination is an important part of Conjure; most workers will tell you that there shouldn't be any type of work done until the worker has done divination on the situation. I work with a couple of tools for divination: cards, blue water, and the bones. I was never taught to read tarot cards, and I am not skilled at them. I have never had any luck in reading them, but if you give me a deck of playing cards or a set of bones, I am on my way.

Bone reading and card reading are very traditional Conjure. In the ole days—and I still do this at times—the client was made to stand on a white cloth and the bones were thrown at their feet on the cloth. This was done so the worker could see what the ailment was and also how to fix it; the bones and the cards are tools for the ancestor to speak through to help the worker in their work.

BONE READING

You can't just gather up a bunch of bones and start throwing them. The bones need to first be treated, and then they need to be dedicated to the ancestors or the spirit you will work with. What does the word "dedicated" mean? This is what webopedia has to say: "Reserved for a specific use. In communications, a dedicated channel is a line reserved exclusively for one type of communication." I never thought of my spiritual link with my ancestors as a "dedicated channel," but I guess it is.

Spirit speaks through the bones or the cards as a way to communicate with me. This might not be the "correct" spiritual term, but it explains exactly what happens when you dedicate your bones to the ancestors. That dedication will open up the lines of communication between you and your ancestors. Sometimes it may be just a feeling, a knowing that you are on track, or you can sometimes hear them speaking in your mind. They communicate with the bones in many different ways; it could be a pattern or the way the bones fall. You must be in tune with your ancestors to be a good bone reader.

Folks throw many different types of bones that they have collected. The bones are collected over time, and possum bones or chicken bones are traditional. Some readers add curios to their

sets, and these are also called bones. Nowadays you can find bones for sale all over the internet, or you can collect them by finding them out in the wild; either way is fine.

The next question is, just how do you dedicate the bones? You could ask fifty workers and almost all of them will tell you something different; but since this is my book, I'm gonna tell you one way I dedicate things to my ancestors. You can use this dedication process for your cards also. Make sure you do a brush-down or spiritual bath before you start any type of work; you don't want to bring the muck you have gathered in your day-to-day dealing with folks to your altar or let it mix with your bones. You should always make it a habit to do at least a brush-down before you do any type of spiritual work no matter how small it may seem.

You may be wondering what in the world is a brush-down or a spiritual bath. I discussed how to make a spiritual wash earlier (see page 36). Follow those directions for making a spiritual bath, too.

A brush-down is a simple but effective way to do a quick cleansing. There are a couple of different tools you can work with: you can buy a small whisk broom, or you can use a candle or a chicken foot.

I'm almost positive I have brought around another question. Why in the world would you use a dried chicken foot? You cleanse with it. Chickens are known for digging and scratching, so the chicken foot is very effective for scratching off blocks, cross conditions, and any other negative thing you might have picked up during your day.

Chicken feet are a big thing in my world, and I hope they will become so in your world, too, for they are one of the best ways to keep cross conditions off and away from your home.

The chicken foot, the candle, and the broom are all worked with the same way: holding the tool in your hand, start at the crown of your head and sweep the tool down and outward in a brushing motion. Please do not go back and forth over your body because all you will be doing is stirring up muck. Move the tool in one long stroke from the crown of your head to the bottom of your feet. Try to do as much of your body as you can. Once the brush-down is done, make sure you dress the crown of your head and the bottom of your feet with some type of blessing oil. You can pray Psalm 23 into a bottle of olive oil and use that as general dressing oil.

A lady stopped me in the middle of a cleansing class a few years ago. She wanted to know where all the junk that was being removed off of folks was going. She informed me that I was not doing the work safely, because I was not teaching them to visualize it going into the earth. Needless to say, I stopped the class so that she could explain to me what she meant. That was something I had never heard of before. I assured her that I knew what I was teaching and I would never teach something that would be harmful. Well, she wasn't done yet. She wanted me to tell her where it went—she just wouldn't let it go—so I simply said, "As you brush down and out, it goes into the earth where you are praying for it to go."

When you remove something by brushing downwards away from you, while praying it to go into Mother Earth for her to heal, then that is where it is gonna go. I just wanted to make sure that was clear in this book so folks can work with ease.

Once the cleansing is complete, it is time to call on your ancestors. Petition them to fill your bones with their power so you will be able to understand what they are saying to you, the message they are trying to communicate to you.

This small setup on your altar is all you need. A setup is a group of candles that are placed in the shape of a cross and the work is set in the center of the setup. Lay your white handkerchief on your ancestor altar or table; spread your bones on top of the hankie. Lay out four candles of your choosing in the shape of a cross around your bones. The first candle goes to the top, the next to the bottom, the next to the left and the last one to the right. The photo here shows this setup, but I moved the bottom candle so you would be able to see the center. This is a basic locking-down setup for many different works. From right to left is opening something up; from left to right is locking something down.

What does "locking down" mean? When you are doing conjure work, there are different layouts that can be worked with. If you are working with the cross setup, then you are either locking something or someone down; in other words you are holding the target in one *place. This can be done with candles, nails, rocks, or anything else that will set up a block. For this work you place the candles from left to right because you are locking something down! That is exactly what you will be doing: locking the power and communication your ancestors share with you into the bones, so the bones retain that power and insight. If you would have placed the candles going from right to left, then you would be opening up the way. You use the opening setup when you are doing works to draw things to you like love, money, a job, or maybe power. There is no limit to the works you can do with either of the setups. Remember: left to right closes and right to left opens.*

You will need to go to your altar daily and repeat this process for seven days. On the eighth day you wrap your bones up in their hankie and you thank your ancestors. Then give them an offering. That part is done, but you're not done just yet.

Take your bones and place them in your pillowcase where you lay your head. Keep them there for seven days. If you have dreams during those seven days, try to write them down. After the seven days are up, lay out your handkerchief. Hold the bones up to your mouth and call on the Trinity first, then your ancestors. Petition them to help you understand the bones; petition them to communicate with you in a way you will understand. Ask a question that you already know the answer too, then throw the bones gently on the handkerchief. Sit there quietly for a few minutes and just study the layout. See if you can understand the message.

Write down what you think you see in the bones, then wait a day and go back. (While you're waiting, you can leave the bones on the altar, tie them back in the hankie, or put them back under their pillow—whatever you feel is best or however

Spirit moves you.) Ask the same questions, and throw the bones again. See how they fall. Don't try too hard because you will block your own insight if you do. Plain and simple there is one thing you cannot do, and that is overthink this or analyze it to death. Like the popular shoe commercial says: "Just Do It!" Trust in your ancestors to help you understand what they are trying to tell you. The very first step is to have a strong connection with your ancestors. They speak through the bones so they can help you with your daily life. This is truly Conjure at its best, because most ole-school workers either throw the bones or read playing cards; they don't usually read tarot cards.

Bone reading is basically like building a puzzle. You as the reader have to find out how the different bones fit together to tell the story. It might not make sense at first; you may even feel a little confused the first few times you throw the bones. Be patient with yourself: bone reading is not something you can ever learn overnight. It's a process that requires a lot of patience, as well as a strong relationship with your ancestors. You will need to develop this skill so you can learn to "discern" what Spirit is really saying to you. This is what makes a true bone reader different from a fake. They follow Spirit and not so much the meanings of the bones.

You start by connecting all the puzzle pieces. When you can do this, then the picture will become clearer. You have to keep pushing at it, and before you know it, the whole puzzle is completed. Bone reading works the same way as putting that puzzle together. Each bone tells its own unique story. The thing to remember is to relax and let Spirit guide you in the reading. Once you learn as a reader how the different bones relate to one another and learn to read the pattern of the bones, then you'll know how to read for a client. Even if they try to hide something from you, the bones will tell it. No one can tell you what Spirit is telling you except you; you know what you feel and see.

You can follow the same instructions above to empower a deck of cards or a pendulum. It is the basic method whenever you need to empower a tool.

PROTECTION DURING A READING

The next thing that is really important when you are doing divination is protection. Anytime we start laying out cards or throwing bones for a client, we are linking our spirit in some small way with theirs. It is important that we keep ourselves cleansed and protected because not everyone you are around in your daily life or who will come to you for guidance does. I have found that most folks outside of Conjure do not worry about doing regular cleansing, much less keeping protection work going. These are two of the most important works you should keep going. Your life would run a lot smoother. I'm gonna share with you some steps I take and that I teach my students.

When you are ready to open a reading for a client, you need a white handkerchief and three candles: a red one, a white one, and a blue one. Let me explain the colors:

* The red one represents the blood of the ancestors that runs through your veins.

* The white candle represents you or the client.

* The blue one is for King Solomon. King Solomon represents wisdom and knowledge. He is very much needed in this type of work.

1. Lay the white hankie out on your reading table, then place the red, white, and blue candles on your reading

table in a straight line. Place the red one on the left, the white one in the center, and the blue one on the right.

2. Carve the client's name on the white candle that is placed in the center. I like to use a rusty nail because not only are nails used to nail things down but the rust on the nail adds extra power.

3. Dress the candles with holy oil.

You can make a simple holy oil by praying Psalm 23 into a new bottle of olive oil. You simply remove the cap and hold the bottle up to your mouth and say the prayer into the bottle.

---

4. Now pick up each candle and hold it up to your mouth.

5. Pray into each candle asking Spirit to open your eyes so that you see clearly:

   Petition your ancestors, as you hold the red candle up to your mouth.

   Call on the Spirit of Discernment as you hold the white candle to your mouth.

   Petition the prophet Solomon as you hold the blue candle to your mouth.

6. After you have prayed over all of the candles, place the photo of the person you are reading for under the white candle. If you're reading for yourself, then your photo will go under the white candle.

7. Spread your bone reading handkerchief in front of the candles and lay your bones on top of the hankie.

8. Light your candles from right to left and start your opening prayers. Knock three times on your reading table and call on your ancestors. Petition your ancestors to come and to only let the truth be known in the reading. This may seem like a simple candle setup, but it is very powerful because you are opening the door for your ancestors to meet you.

9. Now you are ready to read your bones. Pick up your bones in your hands and then hold them up to your mouth so your breath can cover them as you pray 1 Kings 3 V 9–14 over your bones. At this time, you may also add whatever words of wisdom or heartfelt prayer you may have about the reading.

1 KINGS 3 V 9–14

9 SO GIVE YOUR SERVANT A DISCERNING HEART TO GOVERN YOUR PEOPLE AND TO DISTINGUISH BETWEEN RIGHT AND WRONG. FOR WHO IS ABLE TO GOVERN THIS GREAT PEOPLE OF YOURS?"

10 THE LORD WAS PLEASED THAT SOLOMON HAD ASKED FOR THIS.

11 SO GOD SAID TO HIM, "SINCE YOU HAVE ASKED FOR THIS AND NOT FOR LONG LIFE OR WEALTH FOR YOURSELF, NOR HAVE ASKED FOR THE DEATH OF YOUR ENEMIES BUT FOR DIS-CERNMENT IN ADMINISTERING JUSTICE,

12 I WILL DO WHAT YOU HAVE ASKED. I WILL GIVE YOU A WISE AND DISCERNING HEART, SO THAT THERE WILL NEVER HAVE BEEN ANYONE LIKE YOU, NOR WILL THERE EVER BE.

13 MOREOVER, I WILL GIVE YOU WHAT YOU HAVE NOT ASKED FOR—BOTH WEALTH AND HONOR—SO THAT IN YOUR LIFE-TIME YOU WILL HAVE NO EQUAL AMONG KINGS.

14 AND IF YOU WALK IN OBEDIENCE TO ME AND KEEP MY
DECREES AND COMMANDS AS DAVID YOUR FATHER DID, I
WILL GIVE YOU A LONG LIFE."

When you are finished praying over the bones, it is time
to start the reading. Whether you are reading for a client or
yourself, the steps are the same. Hold the bones up close to
the client's mouth and tell them to say their name over the
bones three times and to blow three breaths onto the bones.
By doing this you are letting the bones pick up on the spirit of
the client so they can be read. Then you gently drop the bones
on your white handkerchief. Watch how the bones fall. Then
you continue your reading. Once the reading is over, it is time
to close the door.

For me this is the most important part of the reading, because
you don't want a spirit that might have been drawn to the reading and the power of the prayer and the flame of the candles you
lit hanging around after the reading is done. When the reading
is over, thank your ancestors for sharing their guidance with you
and your client. Pick up your bones and hold them to your mouth
where your petition will flow over them. Petition your ancestors
by praying, "Ancestors, I petition you, just as you woke the bones
up, will you now put them back to sleep so they can rest!"

Then thank the Trinity or your higher power for showing
you the way. Ask that everyone go in peace. Then you call
on Solomon, and thank him for sharing his wisdom with you.
Thank him for standing beside you during the reading. The
next step is to snuff your candles out. Start with the one on the
left now then move across to the right. You opened the door
for Spirit to come in by lighting the candles from right to left;
now you must shut the door and this is done by putting out the
flames from left to right.

After you snuff out the candles, wrap your bones in the white hankie, then place them on your ancestor altar. Each time you do a reading and you work this conjure candle setup, you are building a stronger link between yourself, the bones, and the ancestors.

It is very important that you know how to open and close the gate to the spirits. I was taught that just the act of laying out the cards or throwing the bones is opening the door for spirits to walk through; so it's important to know how to shut that door once it is open.

I want to end this section on throwing the bones with something that you might not know. Did you know that the Bible speaks about the throwing of lots? I'm not sure, but I think in that time it was either stones or sticks that were being thrown. There are multiple references.

Lots were cast or thrown to divine information. This comes straight from the Bible. Throwing lots was a way of finding out information through the Holy Ghost. It is a gift from God.

1 Corinthians 2 V 9–14

9 But as it is written, Eye hath not seen, nor ear heard, neither have entered into the heart of man, the things which God hath prepared for them that love him.

10 But God hath revealed them unto us by his Spirit: for the Spirit searcheth all things, yea, the deep things of God.

11 For what man knoweth the things of a man, save the spirit of man which is in him? even so the things of God knoweth no man, but the Spirit of God.

12 NOW WE HAVE RECEIVED, NOT THE SPIRIT OF THE WORLD, BUT THE SPIRIT WHICH IS OF GOD; THAT WE MIGHT KNOW THE THINGS THAT ARE FREELY GIVEN TO US OF GOD.

13 WHICH THINGS ALSO WE SPEAK, NOT IN THE WORDS WHICH MAN'S WISDOM TEACHETH, BUT WHICH THE HOLY GHOST TEACHETH; COMPARING SPIRITUAL THINGS WITH SPIRITUAL.

14 BUT THE NATURAL MAN RECEIVETH NOT THE THINGS OF THE SPIRIT OF GOD: FOR THEY ARE FOOLISHNESS UNTO HIM: NEITHER CAN HE KNOW THEM, BECAUSE THEY ARE SPIRITU- ALLY DISCERNED.

2 PETER 1 V 19–21

19 WE HAVE ALSO A MORE SURE WORD OF PROPHECY; WHEREUNTO YE DO WELL THAT YE TAKE HEED, AS UNTO A LIGHT THAT SHINETH IN A DARK PLACE, UNTIL THE DAY DAWN, AND THE DAY STAR ARISE IN YOUR HEARTS:

20 KNOWING THIS FIRST, THAT NO PROPHECY OF THE SCRIP- TURE IS OF ANY PRIVATE INTERPRETATION.

21 FOR THE PROPHECY CAME NOT IN OLD TIME BY THE WILL OF MAN: BUT HOLY MEN OF GOD SPAKE AS THEY WERE MOVED BY THE HOLY GHOST.

LEVITICUS 16 V 7–10

7 AND HE SHALL TAKE THE TWO GOATS, AND PRESENT THEM BEFORE THE LORD AT THE DOOR OF THE TABERNACLE OF THE CONGREGATION.

8 AND AARON SHALL CAST LOTS UPON THE TWO GOATS; ONE LOT FOR THE LORD, AND THE OTHER LOT FOR THE SCAPEGOAT.

9 And Aaron shall bring the goat upon which the Lord's lot fell, and offer him for a sin offering.

10 But the goat, on which the lot fell to be the scapegoat, shall be presented alive before the Lord, to make an atonement with him, and to let him go for a scapegoat into the wilderness.

Jonah 1 V 7–15

7 And they said every one to his fellow, Come, and let us cast lots, that we may know for whose cause this evil is upon us. So they cast lots, and the lot fell upon Jonah.

8 Then said they unto him, Tell us, we pray thee, for whose cause this evil is upon us; What is thine occupation? and whence comest thou? what is thy country? and of what people art thou?

9 And he said unto them, I am an Hebrew; and I fear the Lord, the God of heaven, which hath made the sea and the dry land.

10 Then were the men exceedingly afraid, and said unto him. Why hast thou done this? For the men knew that he fled from the presence of the Lord, because he had told them.

11 Then said they unto him, What shall we do unto thee, that the sea may be calm unto us? for the sea wrought, and was tempestuous.

12 And he said unto them, Take me up, and cast me forth into the sea; so shall the sea be calm unto you: for I know that for my sake this great tempest is upon you.

13 NEVERTHELESS THE MEN ROWED HARD TO BRING IT TO THE LAND; BUT THEY COULD NOT: FOR THE SEA WROUGHT, AND WAS TEMPESTUOUS AGAINST THEM.

14 WHEREFORE THEY CRIED UNTO THE LORD, AND SAID, WE BESEECH THEE, O LORD, WE BESEECH THEE, LET US NOT PERISH FOR THIS MAN'S LIFE, AND LAY NOT UPON US INNO-CENT BLOOD: FOR THOU, O LORD, HAST DONE AS IT PLEASED THEE.

15 SO THEY TOOK UP JONAH, AND CAST HIM FORTH INTO THE SEA: AND THE SEA CEASED FROM HER RAGING.

CARD READING

I have shared a lot about bone reading, but I would also like to share some information on reading the cards. If you are unfamiliar with reading cards, there are many books and websites that will explain the meanings of the cards to you. In this book, I will teach you some special techniques that you will not find elsewhere.

There are two spreads I love to work with when doing special readings for clients that I want to share with you.

Holy Trinity Crossroads Spread

This unique spread is powerful because you are combining two works: (1) the power of the Holy Trinity as shown by the pyramid and (2) the crossroads because the base of this spread is four cards, which is where you'll find the answer. This spread is used when you need to find something specific. If you are on the lookout, then this spread will lend a helping hand and lead you to the truth.

Shuffle the playing cards while petitioning God and your ancestors to open your eyes and reveal the truth.

Lay one card down, then lay two cards below the first card, followed by three cards, and then four. This will create a pyramid of four rows with one card at the top and four cards at the bottom. Notice that all cards are doubled for each row after the first.

Read the cards starting at the first row with the top card and continue from there. The first row represents the immediate situation and the emotional impact. It shows what's going on and how you're being affected. The following rows show what you can do about the situation and what will unfold, while the last row shows the answer or solution to your problem. That's how you read the rows.

Your job as a reader is to put all the pieces of the puzzle together because the cards tell a story. Each card has a specific meaning that you have to take into account, but that meaning does change with the other cards surrounding it.

You can't base your whole reading off one or a few cards; instead you have to look at *all* the cards together. When you watch how the cards interplay, you see the story take place as it is.

The top card of the pyramid represents the petitioner, the situation, or circumstance being inquired about in the consultation. The second row shows the effect of the two cards on the top (petitioner) card. If the petitioner card is negative or shows any blocks, look to the second row to see how far the blocks will last. Anytime you see blocked cards in a spread, then look how the other cards will react against those blocks. If the surrounding cards counteract those blocks, then you have nothing to worry about because the block has been canceled out by Spirit. The three cards in the third row show you how the situation plays out while the final row tells you the answer. The four bottom cards show you how you'll get to the solution.

All the cards are important to this spread but the cards you need to really pay attention to are the petitioner and bottom row of cards, since the petitioner shows you in a nutshell what you face, while the bottom cards tell you what to make of the situation and what will come from it. The strongest cards are the base cards because there are four of them, which represent the crossroads. The crossroads is where all our power lies.

If you really pay attention, you'll realize that the pyramid shows your power, starting with the top card and how to build it up with the other cards. The base cards will tell you how successful you'll be or, if blocked, then what/where you need to pay attention to so you can fix the problem.

You are working with the power of the Holy Trinity and the crossroads with this conjure spread, which makes it extremely powerful. You can also incorporate this spread into work with your ancestors. For example, if you want to draw success and have the cards show you what to do, then burn a vigil or conjure lamp on your spread every day while repeating your petition.

This spread is also good for discovering blocks. If you pull a bunch of cards that represent you being blocked or having a crossed condition and the cards aren't counteracted by neighboring cards that represent things turning out in your favor, then here's another spread you can work with to reverse those blocks. A crossed condition or a spiritual block stops you from the success that is yours. Here's an example. Let's say you are trying to buy a new car, but things are going wrong with the paperwork or you might be having an issue getting it financed when there shouldn't be an issue. It has been one thing after another trying to get the car. This is considered a blocked condition.

It could be the spirits trying to protect you from buying a lemon or it could be something else. Either way you need to do a cleansing. It is always important to do a reading in order to try and find out what is causing the issues; then you can do the work that is needed to fix the situation.

Holy Trinity Reversal Spread

If you are feeling blocked up, confused, got a crossed condition, or have discovered through divination that your roads have been blocked, this spread is what you need to remove those blocks and open your roads.

The Holy Trinity Reversal Spread works just like the first one we covered, but it does the opposite. This spread will show you how to remove the block, the impact of the crossed condition on the situation or your life, and if your work will be a total success. In this case, you'll start the pyramid with four cards in the first row and remove a card from each row until the last and final row has only one, which is the petitioner.

The first row points to the block. The four cards will show you the work you need to do to remove or reverse the block. The second row shows how uncrossing work will affect the situation. The cards in that row will tell you how it all plays out in your favor or against you. The third row tells you what'll happen that leads to the final card—the petitioner on the fourth row. Ideally you want that petitioner card in the fourth row to be cleansed and uncrossed because that tells you the work is successful. All the cards starting at the first row lay out the problem, how to fix it, and what will take place to get to the end result with the petitioner card, which will tell you how successful your work is.

It is important that the final card comes out cleansed and uncrossed because that is the petitioner card, which represents your spirit. You don't want your spirit all crossed up and in a jam. The pyramid reversal spread is so strong because you start off at four cards and take one away until it ends up with the one card that is your spirit. As you read the cards, you're removing the block just like with the Walls of Jericho work that can be found in the Bible in Joshua 6. You're also knocking anything down that's put you in a bind because, as you take away each card from the row, you're taking the power away from the block and putting it back in yourself.

If you know what you're doing and you're tricky enough as a worker, you can use this spread in uncrossing work to set you free. Since you're dealing with Spirit, you need to petition your ancestors to destroy those blocks.

Here's a simple but strong work to go along with your card reading.

Ancestor Cleansing

1. First lay out a white prayer cloth onto which you've prayed the Holy Spirit on your working table.

2. Place your photo in the center of the prayer cloth and petition God for help.

3. Make a powder by burning a copy of the photos of your ancestors, and then mix the ash with dirt from a church and a pinch of crossroads dirt and sprinkle the powder on the prayer cloth starting at the photo in the center and going outward towards the edge. Make sure your photo is covered with the powder.

4. Petition your ancestors for protection and to remove any blocks that hold you in a bind. What you're doing is making a spiral that goes counterclockwise to undo any blocks on your spirit.

5. Shuffle your cards and ask the Holy Trinity for insight.

6. Ask your ancestors to fight for you and show you what you need to do in order to remove the crossed condition.

7. Lay out the cards on the prayer cloth on top of the powder in the reversal pyramid.

8. Read the cards and take note to what Spirit is telling you.

9. Cleanse yourself with a white vigil candle starting at the crown of your head and going all the way down to your feet. You may also use a blue vigil instead of white for this work.

10. Light the vigil candle on your prayer cloth and petition God to set you free.

11. If you have really strong blocks on you, then get you a piece of chain or rope and cleanse yourself with that chain from head to toe.

12. Cut the chain in half and wrap the pieces of chain around the vigil candle in the center of your setup.

This work is really powerful and can't fail you.

SPIRITS OF CONJURE

THE SPIRITS OF CONJURE are the ancestors, elders, and spirits that walk with a conjure worker. They are to be uplifted and honored, because without the ancestors this work would not exist and neither would this book. If you seek to do this work, then you must understand the culture of those who first brought this work over here through slavery.

Slavery is not something folks are comfortable talking about. Folks would rather not even acknowledge that it happened—but it *did* happen. So many folks have completely forgotten about these people and what they went through. So many wish to claim Conjure, but without discussing the suffering and the terror that this work comes from.

I have never been one to beat around the bush. My mama warned me when I was a young child to watch out for fast talkers. What folks call Conjure, hoodoo, or rootwork is a way of life for me and my family. I was raised on stories told to me by my mama, sister, and elders. This work is what folks used to call ole wives' tales before the internet put it out there for the world to see. It was not something that was shared and passed around as it is now. It was family traditions or an elder teaching you a few bits of knowledge here and there. It was to be honored and respected, but today it has turned into a moneymaking machine and the ancestors are long forgotten. Those who were captured and brought over here in the bottoms of ships aren't even a memory for some who claim this work. Folks need to remember that anything that has blood shed on it is powerful.

This work has never been about money; it's about the community and helping folks who need help. I've been paid in everything from food to my rooster Houdini, whom I got for a job I did for a fellow who needed help. There is not enough money to buy that rooster from me. It was a good trade.

The point I am trying to make is that folks who are gifted for this work should honor the ancestors and the culture this work comes out of. Folks need to stop trying to add to or take away from this work. It's an insult to the ancestors and to those who are raised in this culture. It doesn't need fixing. Instead, what needs to happen is folks need to understand where this work comes from and go from there. I write books as a way to honor the ancestors and my culture and to help folks learn the work.

If folks don't know how to do the work, I have found they just mix whatever they do know in with the information they have found. I call this mixen and moxen and whitewashing the work. This work is hidden in the whole culture, not just the magic of it. Lessons are learned in the stories that are told to us as children. Works are hidden within some of those stories. The elders were very wise, and the ancestors have never been forgotten. They live on in every lesson learned. Outsiders rarely understand the culture or the work.

Here is an example: Some folks consider the tales of Brer Rabbit and Tar Baby to be racist, but to a child raised in a family where this work is part of their daily lives, those tales hold valuable lessons and conjure secrets. Brer Rabbit has been traced all the way back to Africa from stories told of a Trickster. As children, these stories were told to us to teach lessons we would need as adults. They also show a mindset that most rural Southern children are taught.

For those unfamiliar with Brer Rabbit and Tar Baby, their stories are retold and reclaimed by the African American author and storyteller Julius Lester in his book Tales of Uncle Remus: The Adventures of Brer Rabbit *(Puffin Books, 2006).*

In the story "Brer Rabbit and the Tar Baby," Brer Rabbit's enemy Brer Fox sets a trap for Brer Rabbit by making a dollie called Tar Baby from tar and turpentine. Both of these items are used in Conjure for protection and uncrossing work. Brer Fox hid when he heard Brer Rabbit approach. He was beside himself with excitement; he just knew he had Brer Rabbit this time.

Brer Rabbit comes along and speaks politely to Tar Baby, but of course, Tar Baby can't answer him. Politeness is something all Southern children are taught from a very young age: even if you can't stand someone, you better be polite to them in public. Brer Rabbit addresses Tar Baby two or three times, and then he loses his temper.

I was taught as a young child that if you lose your temper, you can't think clearly, and if you're not thinking clearly, then you are headed for trouble just like Brer Rabbit in this story because he didn't look at the whole picture. Brer Fox was having a good laugh; he knew he had his target. Brer Rabbit totally lost it and demanded that Tar Baby take off her hat and be polite and speak. Brer Rabbit said, "I'll teach ya a lesson," and he swung at Tar Baby and his paw got stuck in the tar. Did he stop and think? No, he had all his paws stuck by the time his temper was high.

Finally Brer Fox jumped out laughing and calling, "I got you now!" Brer Rabbit then realized he was in a mess. While Brer Fox was gloating, Brer Rabbit came up with a plan. "Please don't throw me into the briar patch!" he cried. "Roast me, hang me, do whatever you want to do, but please don't throw me into the briar patch." Like any good conjure worker, Brer Rabbit let his enemy think he had won. Brer Fox flung Brer Rabbit into the briars as hard as he could, and Brer Rabbit let out a horrible scream that made the fur stand up on Brer Fox. Then there was only silence. Brer Fox stood listening waiting for painful sounds of misery to come from the briar bushes, but there was nothing. Then Brer Fox heard someone calling his name. He turned around and looked up the hill. Brer Rabbit was sitting on a log combing the tar out of his fur with a wood chip and looking smug.

Brer Rabbit sang, "I was bred and born in the briar patch, Brer Fox." Briar and thorns of any kind are worked with for protection and binding an enemy. Brer Rabbit teaches us to never underestimate an enemy and to always make sure you keep a cool head. Don't ever jump in with both feet or you might end up like Brer Rabbit or your smugness might have you looking like Brer Fox. As you can see, there is information in here that teaches a child how to act and to always be aware of what is going on around them.

There is also conjure information hidden within the story: tar, turpentine, and briars. All of this comes from the ances-tors and the knowledge they brought with them over on the slave ships. Too often this information has been removed from the lessons of this work because outsiders don't know about or understand the culture.

Storytelling was a big part of my growing up. My mama always made us look at things differently. I've written about a few of the ancestors, but it isn't in any way all of them. You can see the power they had and the pride to try to achieve a freedom which only brought them death. Honor them as you would your own ancestors if you are going to do this work; for without them there would be no work! It is important to remember the ones who struggled for freedom in a time when very few of color were free. Nowadays they are all but forgotten.

Now, let me tell you about some of the ancestors and spirits of Conjure.

The information in this section is inconsistent. Some but not all of these ancestors and spirits have detailed rituals or altars associated with them. I've offered the information where it applies. Please feel free to let Spirit or the ancestors themselves guide you to create personal altars for the others, if you so desire.

HISTORICAL ANCESTORS OF CONJURE

What I am calling the "historical ancestors" are those who fought against the unjustness of slavery, of the wrongness of one man owning another man, or someone who fought against the odds and achieved something that was almost unachievable for a nonwhite. It is important that these great people be remembered and that the power they held within their spirit also be remembered. It is that same power we all hold but most folks don't know how to draw it up when they need that power for success. I hope some of these great ancestors will inspire the reader to try a little harder, push a little harder, as the ancestors of this work did to reach their goal.

Gabriel Prosser

Gabriel (1776–1800), commonly known as Gabriel Prosser, was born on the Thomas Prosser tobacco plantation in Henrico County, Virginia. Gabriel was one of the slave ancestors that were taught to read and write as a child. By the time he was ten years old, he was training to be a blacksmith along with his brother Solomon. There is no information found on their parents, but most of the time a gift like blacksmithing was passed down from father to son, generation to generation. By the time Gabriel was twenty, he was reputedly over six feet tall, a large, broad man. He was a born leader, and he was very intelligent. The elders also saw him as a leader.

Things seemed to go well until 1798, when the elder Mr. Prosser, owner of the plantation, passed away and his twenty-two-year-old son, Thomas Henry Prosser, inherited the plantation. It is said that the younger Prosser was tightfisted and cruel. He began to hire out Gabriel and his brother, so they had more freedom. For those who don't know the term "hired out," it means that even though Gabriel was a slave he was allowed to travel and work for other folks with pay. Not all the folks in Virginia liked the idea of the ancestors being hired out. They thought it was dangerous, but such folks were cheaper to hire than their white counterparts. Even though the state of Virginia tried to stop them from being hired out, it was hard to enforce the law. Gabriel was allowed to hire himself out to others to work. He tended to his own hiring out, so I'm just wondering was there Conjure going on here?

He met and associated with many ancestors who were being held as slaves, as well as free blacks and also white laborers. Even though the free ancestors were discriminated against, they managed to prosper. Just about all the cities in the Southern states passed laws to try and stop free and enslaved ancestors and working-class whites from socializing. This was seen as a threat.

Gabriel had strong feelings against the white slave owners who cheated the slaves they hired to do work; also some of the folks he hung around with had some strong views about the way the lower white folks were treated. I'm sure in those days they would have been called radicals or worse. He dreamed of being free and being able to prosper as a blacksmith.

Gabriel, his brother Solomon, and a fellow named Jupiter stole a pig in September of 1799, and they were caught. The white overseer of the plantation got into it with Gabriel, who bit a large chunk of his ear off. There were laws against blacks putting their hands on white folks, so that crime was punishable by death. Gabriel was found guilty in the white court, but he found a loophole called "benefit of clergy" where he could choose branding over hanging. All he had to do was recite a verse out of the Bible, which he did, and he was branded on the hand in court. He also spent a month in jail. It seemed after that trouble followed him until he rebelled. Gabriel thought if they all rebelled that the poor whites would join them; he planned on capturing Capitol Square in Richmond. When he told his brother and a few other folks what he had planned, they started recruiting folks. Some were free, some were ancestors, and some were whites they bonded together with for freedom. Gabriel was inspired by the battle at Saint-Domingue, where the Haitian slaves won their independence and their nation.

Gabriel and his followers had weapons and were making bullets; they were also making swords. They were spreading out and getting more recruits; the movement was growing. The plan was to move on August 30, 1800. Some area white folks learned about it and told the governor, who just blew it off, but the flooding rains came and so Gabriel and his followers had to postpone it until the next night. Before they could move the next night, two slaves who had been caught broke under the pressure the law and their owners put on them and told what was gonna happen. Governor Monroe called in the white patrols, and they searched the countryside for them until the state militia arrived. By September 9 they had captured thirty slaves, but Gabriel and Jack Ditcher, his right-hand man, remained missing. They were sentenced without a jury by a special court. Thomas Henry Prosser who owned Gabriel brought forth one of his slaves named Ben who told all he knew as did others. Solomon and others were hung.

Gabriel was on the James River when he saw a schooner named *Mary*. Swimming out, he boarded the boat and asked to speak to the captain. There were two blacks on the boat, one named Isham and the other named Billy. The captain was a Richardson Taylor, and he had once been an overseer. Billy knew who Gabriel was and what he had tried to do. The captain agreed to get Gabriel to safety, but when the boat docked in Norfolk, Virginia, Billy went to the law and told them who Gabriel was. It's assumed that he turned him in for the promised three-thousand-dollar reward, but in the end he was given only fifty dollars.

Gabriel Prosser was hung on October 10, 1800. He died alone. He had refused to make any type of statement in court. He simply wanted to be hung alongside the other six that were hung on the same day, but even that was denied him. The state of Virginia had to pay out more than $8,900 to the slave owners as compensation for hanging their slaves. I honor and respect this ancestor.

Mother Sojourner Truth

Every woman in America should honor Mother Sojourner Truth. She battled for women's rights and equal treatment. She was a true warrior for the women's rights movement. She is best known for her speech on racial equality "Ain't I a Woman?" delivered in 1851 at the Ohio Women's Rights Convention.

She was born a slave in New York around 1797. Her birth name was Isabella Baumfree, and she could only speak Dutch. Her parents had twelve children, and the whole family was owned by a Colonel Hardenbergh. The colonel had kept the family together, but when he passed, the whole family then belonged to his son, who separated them and sold them off. Mother Truth was sold on the auction block with a flock of sheep for a hundred dollars. John Neely bought her, and he was a cruel man as she remembered. She was sold twice more in the following two years until she ended up on the property of John Dumont.

During her years with Dumont, she was taught English. She fell in love with a guy from a plantation next to hers and they had two children, but his owner wouldn't let them marry. They were never allowed to see each other again. Dumont forced Mother Truth to marry an elder in approximately 1817. They had three children together: Sophia, Elizabeth, and a son Peter.

On July 4, 1827, slavery was abolished in New York, but Mother Truth had left New York with her daughter Sophia. The other two children had to be left behind. Peter had been sold illegally to a man in Alabama, and when Mother Truth found out, she went before a white court and got her son brought back to New York. This case was the very first where a black woman had successfully won a court case in America.

Mother Truth worked for a preacher named Elijah Pierson in 1829 for a while. Then she worked for a man named Prophet Matthias. It soon came to light that the Prophet Matthias was a con man, and shortly after they left Elijah Pierson's home, Elijah passed away. Believe it or not Prophet Matthias was accused of poisoning him. He and a couple who followed him, "the Folgers," tried to implicate Mother Truth in the crime. Prophet Matthias was eventually let go for lack of evidence. The Folgers were brought to court by Mother Truth in 1835, and she won a slander suit against them.

In 1844, she joined the Northampton Association of Education and Industry in Northampton, Massachusetts. The association had been founded by abolitionists for the reform of women's rights. All the members lived together on five hundred acres. Mother Truth met William Lloyd Garrison, Frederick Douglass, and David Ruggles there. The community broke up in 1846, but Mother Truth was just getting started as a reformer and activist. She was right up there with Mama Moses. Some folks saw her as a radical, but as she became more well known, she drew larger and hospitable crowds. She fought for equal rights for all women and civil rights for all blacks. She fought for black and white women to have equal rights.

Mother Truth spoke with President Abraham Lincoln about her beliefs and her experience; she also encouraged her grandson, James Caldwell, to enlist in the service. She was bold and had a backbone of steel. In 1865—*years* before Mother Rosa Parks—Mother Truth attempted to ride in a Washington streetcar that was designated for white folks. For many years, she battled Congress for land grants for elders who were former slaves, but she was never successful. She passed away November 26, 1883, at her home in Battle Creek, Michigan.

Nat Turner

Nat Turner was an educated man who could read and write; he was also gifted with the sight. He was born on October 2, 1800, in Jerusalem, Virginia. His given name was Nathaniel Turner. He had a strong faith, and he believed God had sent him to free the ancestors from slavery. He had three visions that proved this to him. He was a man of God and a strong spiritual leader. Many ancestors looked up to him and trusted him and his mission. Most had known him since he was a young man, and they knew how gifted he was. He prayed often, fasted, and read his Bible.

There were four others he trusted and told his plan to. They trusted him and knew Spirit was guiding him to help set them free; they were just waiting for Spirit to give them the go-ahead. The sign finally came when there was an eclipse in the spring of 1831, but Nat became ill and so the plans had to be canceled. They waited for another sign, and on August the 13th of that year the new sign came. Nat noticed that the sun appeared to be blue that day, and so a week later on August 21st it began. Nat and his group of men killed the plantation owner and his whole family while they slept. They then went from plantation to plantation killing every white person they came in contact with. Many others joined him, as they wanted their freedom. There were at least fifty in his army.

Nat and his men were headed to Jerusalem, but they were ambushed. They had killed sixty whites who were slave owners, and they had planned to kill more and take their weapons. Nat got away. He stayed in the woods near his former plantation hiding out; he hid for six weeks. But after that they caught him, and he died on November 11, 1831. They tried him in court, and then they hung him and skinned him. White folks angry over the killing of the other white folks tormented and murdered over two hundred black people, free and enslaved—men, women, and children. The state decided to limit the movements and the education of the ancestors after the uprising.

Nat Turner's revolt was the only slave rebellion on American land to be successful. He sowed the seed of fear that then ran rampant throughout the South. Folks feared that others would pick up the battle again. Here again we find a gifted man of God battling for freedom. No one can deny he was a conjure man who had visions and trusted them. He simply wanted to be free as all of us do. Honor and respect to this ancestor.

Charles Deslondes

Charles Deslondes was a mulatto from Haiti who started a revolt in New Orleans in 1811. There is very little written about him although there were a few newspaper articles on him at the time. It's almost as if history forgot this great ancestor existed. He led five hundred African slaves who were well organized. They were armed with hoes, a few firearms, and axes. They marched into the city from a plantation in German Coast County. They say the plantation was around thirty-six miles from town. They attacked the Andry Plantation, killing the owner's son, before they moved on to meet up with more ancestors. Within hours it is said that folks from all around the area started pouring into New Orleans when they heard of the revolt.

They marched down along the river towards New Orleans, attacking plantations as they went. They had flags flying and were beating drums. When they reached the Trepagnier Plantation, they killed the owner, Mr. Trepagnier, then they moved on and by the next afternoon they had made it to the Jacques Fortier plantation. They killed chickens, cooking and eating them and drinking. Manuel Andry, who had lost his son in the revolt, gathered up eighty troops and started out after the ancestors. They found them at the Francois Bernard Bernoudi plantation and attacked them.

On January 11th, Charles Deslondes was dead and the battle was over. General Wade Hampton reported that sixty were killed and sixteen were captured for trial. The trial was fast and the judgments swift. Twenty-one of the ancestors were placed on poles along the German Coast. Three were found innocent of charges, and six just fell through the cracks and got away—no one knows what happened to them. Court records hold additional details. They identify Charles Deslondes as the head of the group and an ancestor named Black Zenon as the main rebel. These ancestors gave their lives for freedom in a time when it was ok by the world for one man to own another. They should be uplifted with prayer and light.

Harriet "Mama Moses" Tubman

I didn't want to write the same ole historical information about "Mama Moses" that you can find in any Google search; so I contacted Witchdoctor Utu, an authority on Mama Moses, and asked him if he would share some of his knowledge with me. As you will see, he was gracious enough to share some information with me that is not really in circulation. Mama Moses is such a strong ancestor and she did so much to help others gain their freedom I wanted her to have a special place in this book. My many thanks to Witchdoctor Utu for his help in making this the special section I wanted it to be.

Harriet Tubman was born around 1820; she was a field hand and servant. She was descended from Ashanti people.

Because of a severe blow to her head, Mama Moses developed epileptic seizures, but this didn't stop her. After her own escape from slavery, she would spend the next ten years returning to the South to help other slaves reach freedom. It is obvious that she had the sight and was crowned by God, and not only that, but she was very clever and cunning. She had a determination and a strong will, and it shows with all she accomplished. She made at least nineteen trips back to the South. Like many of the ancestors, she attributed her success to her faith in God. She was blessed with prophetic dreams that helped lead her on the paths she would travel on her journeys; she knew where the traps were. She was a small woman, and in a man's world back then I am sure they underestimated her skill and her power.

Although many now try to deny it, Harriet Tubman was a conjure woman and very gifted. It is well known that she treated folks with herbal remedies and healing works. She served in the Union army as a nurse, cook, and scout. Mama Moses was sent to Florida at one point to help with the plague. Folks who were interviewed in St. Catharine's in 1860 believed that she had supernatural powers. She would walk in the graveyard around midnight praying and gathering roots and herbs. Yes, Mama Moses was indeed a Christian; she was just not a mainstream Christian, being more of the conjure worker type.

John Brown, whom so many consider a martyr, went to St. Catherine's to visit with Mama Moses where she was living. She conducted all her business out of her home. He wanted her blessings and for her to help him recruit folks for his raid on Harpers Ferry. He stayed about two weeks with her. She had planned on helping him with the raid; she shared her knowledge with him. Everything was planned out for victory! Or was it?

Captain Brown had a strong respect for Mama Moses, so much so that he dubbed her a general. No one really knows why she missed the raid at Harpers Ferry, but she lived on to save many more of her people. She would come to be known by many names in her lifetime, but for me "Mama Moses" says it all! Like Moses in the Bible she gave her life to getting her people to freedom. Just like in Exodus 9 V 1 when God told Moses to tell Pharaoh to let his people go, she had that same calling.

Exodus 9 V 1

1 Then the Lord said unto Moses, Go in unto Pharaoh, and tell him, Thus saith the Lord God of the Hebrews, Let my people go, that they may serve me.

Harriet Tubman was known as Mama Moses and sometimes Black Moses, but her favorite name was "General Tubman," the title given to her by Captain John Brown. When you look at her life, you can see how respected she was, how folks depended on her for her healing skills, for her wisdom, and for the spiritual power God had gifted her with. Not only was she depended upon for the spiritual needs of others, she was also in charge of protecting those that moved with her along the freedom rails of the Underground Railroad. She could shoot as good as any man. She not only had to defend her charges against slavers, but also bounty hunters because there was a large bounty on her head. There was also the issue of other runaway slaves who didn't always mean well. She was an all-around warrior woman!

When Captain Brown was leaving with his army, he turned to Mama and said to her that if he ever needed her, he would call her name "General Tubman" three times. She was so moved by this declaration that she gave her permission for him to do so. If you feel you need her help, then you simply have to call on three times, too: "General Tubman, General Tubman, and General Tubman." Since Mama Moses was a warrior, healer, strategist, and soldier, you can petition her for a multitude of needs. She was a very gifted seer, so she could also be petitioned to help find information that is hidden.

If you want to set a space up for her and her followers, who stayed by her side until the end, you can build a Cross and Cairn in her honor. This is what Utu has to say about the Cross and Cairn: "It symbolizes the graves of many who were not only lost en route, but actually buried under while free in Canada. A simple cairn and cross was the grave left to mark where their bodies lay, and this is why so many of them have become forgotten or lost to ruin."

It is basically an outside altar where prayers and offerings can be left. Mama Moses accepts many kinds of offerings, but not all! It is said she loved corn bread! She also liked black coffee but detested alcohol of any kind, and so that should never be offered to her. Cool water, tea, and flowers are all welcome on the altar. In her honor you can sing ole spirituals such as "Oh Freedom," "Follow the Drinking Gourd," and "Go Down Moses." You can also read from the book of Exodus.

Build Your Own Cairn and Cross

To build your own Cairn and Cross, find a spot in your yard. Make the cross and bless it. Place the cross in the yard, and build a pile of rocks around it. Pray over the altar. Call on Mama Moses and the spirits that walk with her. Petition her to come and sit on the altar. Dedicate the Cairn and Cross to the souls that have been lost and lay in the ground that we walk upon. Sing ole spirituals and pray from the Old Testament. The spirit of the Cairn and Cross will link with all those built around the world. It will become a power place.

General Tubman Prayer

General Tubman, General Tubman, General Tubman!
Mama Moses, who led so many to freedom,
I ask for your blessings and powers to unshackle me from that which
    binds me,
Free me of those obstacles that hinder my growth.
Bless me, Mama Moses, as I gaze upon the North Star, your celestial
gate and shining mystery, always present in the night sky.
May my roads always lead to freedom and may I never be enslaved.
Lend me your powers of healing and perseverance, cunning, and
    Conjure.
May peace always be upon you and may my prayers be heard.
Amen.

Gullah Jack

Jack Pritchard and Denmark Vesey have a special place in American history. You can't talk about one without talking about the other. They organized what would have been one of the largest slave uprisings in American history, if they hadn't been betrayed.

Denmark Vesey was a literate slave in Charleston, South Carolina, who purchased his own freedom for $600. He helped organize the African Methodist Episcopal (AME) church where he lived. Like many African American leaders of his time, Denmark was a devout Christian who believed in the Holy Trinity and the power of scripture; however, he practiced a different type of Christianity that was unlike the slave masters' religion.

Vesey worked with the book of Exodus and taught the Old Testament out of his home. He preached that the enslaved children of Africa were God's Chosen people like the Hebrews and that they have a birthright to be free. His theology inspired hundreds of slaves, if not thousands, which allowed him to incite a slave rebellion with the help of Gullah Jack.

Gullah Jack, a well-known and highly feared conjure worker and spiritual leader, was born in Angola. Little is known of his early life, other than he was shipped to America from Zanzibar as a slave. Like Denmark Vesey, Gullah Jack wanted to give his enslaved and oppressed kin a taste of freedom. Denmark enlisted Gullah Jack's assistance for the planned rebellion. Through Gullah Jack, thousands of enslaved bondsmen joined the ranks for Denmark's rebellion, bringing the number to a total of nine thousand.

Gullah Jack and Denmark Vesey worked hand in hand to carry out their revolt set for July 14th, the same day that had launched the French Revolution. While Denmark led prayers and teachings out of the Old Testament, fueling the fire of rebellion in the hearts of Charleston's slaves, Gullah Jack worked strong roots and Conjure to reassure his people that all involved would be protected and spared, out of harm's way. Gullah Jack's power as a two-headed worker was so feared that throughout most of the planning no one said a word, until just a month before the rebellion, when the plot was leaked by other slaves, who may or may not have been coerced. Denmark Vesey and Gullah Jack Pritchard were tried in court and executed, along with thirty-four other conspirators.

Denmark Vesey and Gullah Jack were both devout men, who fused their Christian beliefs with African culture and traditions in ways that empowered them and their followers.

Gullah Jack gave his followers crab claws to carry. He advised them to hold the claw to their mouths when the uprising began. Pay close attention and you will see that this is a strong work for protection and overcoming enemies.

Crabs are strong little animals. They have a hard shell, and their pinch can be ferocious. We also see the power of the spoken word if you peel back the layers of the story and pay attention.

From a traditional conjure point of view this simple work with the crab claw makes a lot of sense, so I thought it would be a good idea to share this simple but powerful work with y'all.

Claw Work

Write your petition on your photo or a photo of a target and burn the photo to ash. Load the crab claw with the ash from your photo, a pinch of angelica root, gunpowder, Master of the Woods, and licorice root. Seal the opening of the claw with red wax. Place the loaded crab claw in a cross setup of candles in which you will place the candles in the order of top to bottom, right to left, then you light them in the same order you set them down in. (See details for this candle setup in the Divination chapter.)

Pray over and work your setup for at least five days and carry that little claw with you.

If you are under attack, this little work will move your enemies to the side and far away. It is a triple action work because your spirit is locked down inside the hard shell of the claw for protection while the claw itself nails down your enemies. Then we can't forget that crabs move backwards and side to side, which is what we want our enemies to do so they can move along to the side while we move straight ahead to name and claim our blessings. God bless and honor to all the ancestors who died and suffered for conjure work to be here today. Amen.

Mary Fields aka Black Mary aka Stagecoach Mary

Mary Fields was born in slavery in 1832, but she made her way to freedom and made history. It is said that she was over six feet tall and she could shoot as well as any man. She was a legend in her own time. Folks say she could fight as well as any man, she loved whiskey and smoked cigars, she toted a ten-gauge shotgun and wore a pair of six-shooters. She worked and made her own way in a time when no women had rights, much less a black woman on her own. In 1884 she made her way to Cascade County in Montana. She was looking for a better life. Her first job was at St. Peter's mission where she worked for the Ursuline nuns. She did all the heavy work and hauling. She did a little of everything from chopping wood to carpentry. She would also make supply runs to Helena and Great Falls.

She became a legend, and like all legends, there have been plenty of tales told about her. She lost her job at the mission for being in a gunfight as the story goes, so she found herself out of a job and a place to live. She tried her hand at cooking and opened up a small restaurant, but that soon closed because she didn't have the best cooking skills. Not all the legend was folktales; the fact is in 1895 she became a mail carrier for the United States Post Office. She had always liked her independence so this was just the right job for her, and she was good at it. She had a reputation of getting the mail delivered no matter the conditions of the weather or how far in the mountains she had to go. She and her mule Moses would travel to remote miners' cabins as well as to far outposts. Rain, sleet, snow, or raging heat wouldn't stop her from getting the mail through. She got little credit for her efforts.

She was in her mid-sixties when she stopped carrying the mail; it just became too much for her. She still needed money to live on, so at that age it's said she opened up a laundry in town. She passed away in 1914 of liver failure; a simple cross marks her grave at Hillside Cemetery in Cascade. She is a woman for all women to admire. She was the first African American woman to carry mail and the second woman to work for the postal service. It's said that when the law passed in Montana that women couldn't go into saloons, the mayor gave her permission to enter. She was so very well known and respected.

Aunt Caroline Dye

Aunt Caroline Tracy Dye was a descendant of the Gullah people born somewhere around 1843–46 on the CC Tracy Plantation in Spartanburg, South Carolina. She spent her early years as a house servant. Some folks claim that she belonged to William Tracy, but according to the South Carolina Wills and Probate Records, Mr. William Tracy was deceased in 1842, so it is not possible that he owned her. Mr. CC Tracy was his uncle, and it is assumed that he transferred Caroline to William Tracy's wife, Nancy Griffin Reynolds Tracy. This explains who owned Caroline when she was a slave. So many old plantation records have been lost or destroyed that the information about her is sketchy. At some point Caroline traveled with Nancy Griffin Reynolds Tracy and her children to Arkansas. This would have been around 1860 or 1861. Mrs. Tracy passed away in 1861. It would seem, even though there is no record of it, that Caroline was freed either before Mrs. Tracy's death or right after her death.

Caroline married Martin Dye in Arkansas. It is said that she adopted a lot of his family as her own. She had only one child of her own: a daughter name Hannah. Aunt Caroline was known for her gift of sight as a child, but when she moved to Arkansas, her fame grew. She was a very gifted reader with the playing cards, and she was a healer. She was a devout Christian as well. Many times over she offered money to the local church to help with repairs and such, but the church always refused her kind gesture because of the type of work she did. Folks say when she passed, she was very rich, not only in fame but also in money. They say that she had so many clients coming to her home that she had to hire a cook so she could feed them all while they were waiting for their readings. There are many songs written about her and her gifts. She was a powerful gifted worker and one that should be honored. She is buried in Gum Grove Cemetery in Newport, Arkansas, next to her husband, Martin.

If you would like to set up a small space for Aunt Caroline, you need some haunt blue material; this light blue color represents water in the Gullah culture. As Caroline was part of the Gullah Nation, this would be a good color, as it is something she would have been familiar with. There is a photo of Caroline Dye which you can find all over the internet, so you can easily print out an image of her.

You will also need a new deck of cards, a cross, and a Bible. Set the altar up and set her photo to the left side and the Bible to the right side of her deck of cards in the center of the altar. Set the candle on top of the cards and call her. Invite her to sit on the altar and petition her to fill the deck of cards with her wisdom and her gift of sight so that you may help those who come to you. Give her a cool glass of water. Go back to the altar as long as the candle is burning and pray your petition.

When the candle burns out, pick up the deck of cards, hold them up to your mouth, and then you blow three breaths on the deck and shuffle the cards. Ask a question about something you already know the answer to, then lay out the cards. If the cards read true, they are ready, but if they don't, then you need to repeat the process.

SPIRITUAL ANCESTORS OF CONJURE

Big Mama

The Big Mama family of spirits derives from the archetypal Big Mama, the house slave, who served as the mother over the plantation house. Although in life these brave women had names, those were rarely recorded and are now mostly unknown. Their spirits survive as important and sacred ancestors of Conjure, where they are called Big Mama. Never call them by that disrespectful name, "Mammy." Aunt Jemima is a representation of a Big Mama.

Back in slavery days, it was Big Mama's job to take care of the house and everyone in it. She did all the treating of the ill. She had to cook, clean, let white babies suckle at her breast, and wait on folks hand and foot. Big Mama did what she had to do, which takes a very strong spirit and faith that most folks don't possess. Many Big Mamas also had spiritual gifts: they were gifted healers and card readers. Big Mama is the patron of card readers and healers. You should remember and honor her, even if you just read cards.

The caricature of "Mammy" during slavery and continuing through the era of Jim Crow was used to brainwash white America into thinking that the African American woman was happy cooking, cleaning, and being in service to the white folks. This implied that these ancestors were more than happy and more than willing to be slaves. It is insulting, degrading, hurtful, and obnoxious to think that privileged white Americans really thought they had the right to degrade a woman so. These actions have caused many black folks to hate and despise the image of Big Mama and with good cause.

I feel so blessed that my own mama could see beyond that stereotype. She taught me to see Big Mama as someone who had intelligence, power, cunning, and a strong backbone. To this day, Big Mama is a big part of my life. Big Mama is a powerhouse. She is very wise when it comes to family affairs. She is full of knowledge of roots and herbs, of healing, and of maneuvering around authorities. She has the wisdom to help you see what is missing or being hidden.

Big Mama should be honored and held in high esteem. To honor her will draw great power into your life. If you feel drawn to Big Mama and would like to set up a space for her, so that you can honor her and uplift her spirit, then you need a few items, although you can also just light a red or white candle for her and say some prayers. If you decide to set her up on an altar space, then you need a statue or something to represent her. If you are gifted at dollie making, then you can make a dollie to represent her.

To honor her, you need to place her image in a large cast-iron pot, the kind that the elders used to cook with over an open fire. Iron is almost indestructible, and so she is basically housed in a fortress. The iron pot is also forged by fire so that also adds power to her home.

Big Mama has many tools that she works with to remove crossed conditions and blocks. The broom is one of her favorite tools, as is the machete. Each one of them can be worked with when doing cleansings, protection works, and cut and clear works. One of her favorite offerings is molasses. She is the only spirit that I give molasses to as an offer since molasses is usually worked with when you want to slow down a target. That is except when it is given to Big Mama as an offering.

Give your Big Mama her own deck of cards and a set of bones; she will work with both of them to help you find the answers you are seeking. When I can't find the answer to a situation, I borrow her deck of cards or set of bones to read with. Most of the time everything becomes crystal clear and I find the answer I am looking for. She will bless and empower you as she has so many others.

Big Mama needs her own cast-iron pot, a new deck of cards, a whisk broom, a candle, chalk, a bowl of molasses, some dirt from the four corners of your property, and some type of blade.

* The blade puts the power of defense and cleansing in her hands.
* The cast-iron pot is her fortress and home.
* The cards are for her so that she can communicate with you.
* The broom is for cleansings and protection.
* The candle is to give light to her spirit.
* The chalk is to mark the pot by putting a cross in the bottom of the pot where Big Mama will sit to nail down the power. (Instructions to follow.)
* The molasses and whiskey are to feed her.
* The dirt from the four corners of your property is given to invite her into your home. You are giving her the property to protect and nurture and to make her home.

You can also give Big Mama five tealights and some whiskey steeped with dried red peppers.

There are many Big Mama spirits. Each one may have a different personality. You won't know which spirit and personality has come to you until you start to work with her. I work with a couple of different ones, and each one's power feels different.

Big Mama will draw you towards the things she needs or desires in her pot, so just start out slowly and don't overthink it. Once you have everything together, make sure you cleanse the tools you can with cool running water:

Cleanse the broom under cool running water, then allow it to air-dry. Once the broom has dried, sprinkle a little salt over the head of the broom. Similarly, clean and air-dry her cast-iron pot. Then use the chalk to make a cross in the bottom of the pot. Now make a small cross on each of the arms of that cross.

On each marking of the cross, respectfully call Big Mama and invite her into the pot. Next take the dirt from the four corners of your property and put it over the cross; then take the five tealights and set them in a cross setup. You light them in whichever order you set them down. Repeat your prayers for her and your petition to invite her into your home. I offer you a petition below or you can use one of your own.

Petition

> I call on God the Father, God the Son, and God the Holy Spirit,
> I call on Big Mama, I ask, mother, that you come and sit with me,
> I honor your power of motherhood, your suffering and giving spirit,
> I honor you in this place and time that you may never be forgotten,
> I call to you, Big Mama, come and rest, I call to you, Big Mama, come and rest, I call to you, Big Mama, come and rest!

In the name of God the Father, God the Son, and God the Holy Spirit,
In the name of Big Mama, I greet you with love and joy!

Say the prayers and petition over the candles until they burn out. Once the candles have burned out, you can place her in her new home. You need to repeat your prayers and petition to her as you add each item to her home. The last thing you give her is the whiskey and the molasses with the candle. Take some of the dirt from your property and sprinkle it into the molasses while saying your prayers, then pour a little whiskey into the bowl, then you place the candle into the bowl and light it. If her pot is large enough, you can set the offering inside the pot. If it isn't large enough, then just set the offering in front of the pot. Through the years of honoring and working with her I have found that she likes to have a candle burning in her pot. She needs her own candle to do her work, whatever that may be. She is a wonderful loving spirit, but she can be heavy-handed and "tough" at times. Honor her well and you will be blessed for it.

Cephas/Saint Peter

Cephas means "rock" in Aramaic, the language of Jesus. In most versions of the New Testament, Cephas is translated into the Greek Peter. I include it here in honor of my granddaddy, whose nickname was Cephas, and also because I think that it is important for folks to know.

Feast Day June 29th

St. Peter was one of the first disciples, and he was a hot mess. He was very outspoken, even brash at times. He was not only one of Jesus's favorites, but they were also very good friends. Peter was very strong-willed; maybe this had something to with Jesus choosing him to be part of the foundation of the church. If you look at Galatians 2 V 9, you will see that James, Cephas, and John were perceived as the pillars of the church.

GALATIANS 2 V 9

9 AND WHEN JAMES, CEPHAS, AND JOHN, WHO SEEMED TO BE PILLARS, PERCEIVED THE GRACE THAT WAS GIVEN UNTO ME, THEY GAVE TO ME AND BARNABAS THE RIGHT HANDS OF FELLOWSHIP; THAT WE SHOULD GO UNTO THE HEATHEN, AND THEY UNTO THE CIRCUMCISION.

Some folks claim that saints are all sugary and nice. I'm not sure I believe that. In Acts 5 V 1–11 we see that St. Peter killed a husband and his wife because they lied about the price they sold their land for. To say that he is not dangerous to work with is just silly. He is very powerful and was given the power to bind things in heaven. Look at Matthew 16 V 19, which says that whatever Peter binds on Earth is also bound in heaven. So to me that means whatever work he does on Earth can't be undone because it is also bound in heaven.

MATTHEW 16 V 19

19 AND I WILL GIVE UNTO THEE THE KEYS OF THE KING-DOM OF HEAVEN: AND WHATSOEVER THOU SHALT BIND ON EARTH SHALL BE BOUND IN HEAVEN: AND WHATSO-EVER THOU SHALT LOOSE ON EARTH SHALL BE LOOSED IN HEAVEN.

All door-opening works or crossroads work can be given to St. Peter. This means that anything you need to draw or to remove or block from your life can be given to St Peter. In the ole days, folks would get a picture of him and place it behind their door. If you want to work with St. Peter, you can just print out a copy of his picture off the internet. I have found that the one of him upside down on the cross works best. Some folks think he is the devil and that is why he was crucified upside down, but that is absolutely not true. He was crucified upside down because he didn't feel he was worthy to be hung upright like Jesus was. I work with him a lot on many different issues, and he has never let me down.

Moses: God's Two-Headed Worker

Moses has been regarded as one of the most powerful conjure workers ever born. Since the days of slavery, conjure workers have looked to him for power and guidance because Moses spoke directly to God. He is the only living person who was allowed to see God. He was allowed to see God's back. Because of his faith in God and the fact that he allowed God to use him to help his people, Moses was ordained with many gifts through which miracles took place. God used Moses to restore faith in his people and lead them to the Promised Land. Moses had a lot of trials and tribulations in his life. Right from the beginning in Exodus 2 it tells the story of how his mama had to place him in a small boat and put him in the reeds so he wouldn't be found.

EXODUS 2 V 1–4

1 AND A MAN OF THE HOUSE OF LEVI WENT AND TOOK AS WIFE A DAUGHTER OF LEVI.

2 SO THE WOMAN CONCEIVED AND BORE A SON. AND WHEN SHE SAW THAT HE WAS A BEAUTIFUL CHILD, SHE HID HIM THREE MONTHS.

3 BUT WHEN SHE COULD NO LONGER HIDE HIM, SHE TOOK AN ARK OF BULRUSHES FOR HIM, DAUBED IT WITH ASPHALT AND PITCH, PUT THE CHILD IN IT, AND LAID IT IN THE REEDS BY THE RIVER'S BANK.

4 AND HIS SISTER STOOD AFAR OFF, TO KNOW WHAT WOULD BE DONE TO HIM.

He refused to claim Pharaoh's daughter as his mother, as you can read in Hebrews 11 V 24–25.

HEBREWS 11 V 24–25

24 BY FAITH MOSES, WHEN HE WAS COME TO YEARS, REFUSED TO BE CALLED THE SON OF PHARAOH'S DAUGHTER;

25 CHOOSING RATHER TO SUFFER AFFLICTION WITH THE PEOPLE OF GOD, THAN TO ENJOY THE PLEASURES OF SIN FOR A SEASON.

Of course, this started a whole big mess. Moses was gifted by God to have the power of faith and prayer. Pharaoh wouldn't give up and was constantly going against God's law.

Moses had a throw-down with Pharaoh's magicians because they challenged God's authority. Moses, like all God's folks, had a mission assigned to him by the Spirit of God. Moses was sent by God to deliver his people and set them free. He worked his conjure stick to hammer Pharaoh and his army. By his calling on God, Moses's conjure stick turned into a snake and swallowed the rods of Pharaoh's magicians, which had also turned to snakes. This tells us that Moses can defeat any enemy known or unknown.

Moses can be petitioned for any situation where you need a helping hand. If you feel defeated or left out in the desert—or maybe you feel deserted—Moses is the one to petition and call for help. He will lead you out of despair into the land of milk and honey.

The Prophet Elijah

Elijah is one of God's very powerful prophets. God gave Elijah the power to take a life or to bring the dead back to life. God also gave Elijah the power to make fire fall from the sky. The ole folks will tell you that Elijah rode a flaming chariot and horses to heaven. In 2 Kings it tells us that Elijah was with his son when God called Elijah home.

2 KINGS 2 V 8–11

8 AND ELIJAH TOOK HIS MANTLE, AND WRAPPED IT TOGETHER, AND SMOTE THE WATERS, AND THEY WERE DIVIDED HITHER AND THITHER, SO THAT THEY TWO WENT OVER ON DRY GROUND.

9 AND IT CAME TO PASS, WHEN THEY WERE GONE OVER, THAT ELIJAH SAID UNTO ELISHA, ASK WHAT I SHALL DO FOR THEE, BEFORE I BE TAKEN AWAY FROM THEE. AND ELISHA SAID, I PRAY THEE, LET A DOUBLE PORTION OF THY SPIRIT BE UPON ME.

10 AND HE SAID, THOU HAST ASKED A HARD THING: NEVER-THELESS, IF THOU SEE ME WHEN I AM TAKEN FROM THEE, IT SHALL BE SO UNTO THEE; BUT IF NOT, IT SHALL NOT BE SO.

11 AND IT CAME TO PASS, AS THEY STILL WENT ON, AND TALKED, THAT, BEHOLD, THERE APPEARED A CHARIOT OF FIRE, AND HORSES OF FIRE, AND PARTED THEM BOTH ASUN-DER; AND ELIJAH WENT UP BY A WHIRLWIND INTO HEAVEN.

In 1 Kings 17 we are told that when God brought the great drought on the land, the ravens kept Elijah alive while he was waiting on God to decide what to do. God said, "3 Get away from here and turn eastward, and hide by the Brook Cherith, which flows into the Jordan. 4 And it will be that you shall drink from the brook, and I have commanded the ravens to feed you there." He trusted God with an undeniable faith; even when there was no food or water, his faith that God would take care of him never wavered.

This whole thing started because Jezebel, who was King Ahab's wife, began to order the death of God's prophets. Of course, God didn't appreciate this, so he sent Elijah in. King Ahab wouldn't listen to God, though, so God ordered a drought—no rain in sight. The problem with Jezebel was she worshipped the god Baal. She didn't like Elijah talking about his God and how powerful he is, so in 1 Kings we see she sent him a challenge, which he gladly picked up.

1 KINGS 19 V 1–2

1 AND AHAB TOLD JEZEBEL ALL THAT ELIJAH HAD DONE, AND WITHAL HOW HE HAD SLAIN ALL THE PROPHETS [OF BAAL] WITH THE SWORD.

2 THEN JEZEBEL SENT A MESSENGER UNTO ELIJAH, SAYING, SO LET THE GODS DO TO ME, AND MORE ALSO, IF I MAKE NOT THY LIFE AS THE LIFE OF ONE OF THEM BY TOMORROW ABOUT THIS TIME.

The battle was on. He accepts the challenge, and not only does he offer to battle Jezebel, he also battles her priest and her god Baal. Want to know what happens next? Check out 1 Kings and 2 Kings!

The Prophet Elijah is like a double-edged sword: he can be gentle, as he was with the widow who fed him, or he can bring fire raining from the sky. He will serve up justice with his mighty sword and defend you against your enemies.

The Queen of the Waters

When I was young, my mama and my oldest sister used to tell me stories of the Queen of the Waters. She ruled over everything in the waters, and sometimes she would take to humans if she thought they were hers. I was first told of her when I was about twelve or thirteen and almost drowned in the river.

I am a Leo, which is a fire sign, but my whole life I have loved the water. When I was a child, in the summertime I lived at the pool, or if we went camping, which we did often in the summer, I loved the river or the beach. I still do.

The water to me is empowering and relaxing at the same time. I feel at home in the water even though I am a fire sign. I wasn't going to write about Momi, the Queen of the Waters, because it is so personal, but I feel it is a story worth telling.

One summer we went camping for a few weeks. My mama loved to fish and be outdoors. I was taught at a young age to fish and hunt. I can skin a deer and clean fish. This one summer I remember because I almost drowned. There was a family camped next to ours, and they had two boys. I can't remember the younger boy's name, but I will never forget the older boy's name. His name was Sid. We became fast friends and would swim until our parents made us get out of the water.

There was a small island across the way from where we were camped, and so we had been swimming back and forth just playing around. I have always been a good swimmer, and I am safe around water. I respect it. This would be our last swim to the island.

We swam to the island racing; I was over halfway back when I heard Sid. I turned around, and he was fighting the water to keep himself up. I swam back to him and got ahold of him. He was so panicked until he was pushing me down under the water. To this day I remember looking towards the shore and seeing my mama standing there. Then I was being pushed under the water again. All I could think of was my mama.

Right when I thought I was going to drown, something pushed me up out of the water! Sid was turned with his back to me, and I was swimming with him in tow. I was so scared. My mama was crying, standing there in the water. His parents came out into the water and got him. I made my way to my mama, and she was saying, "Thank you, thank you!"

Mama said, "She saved you!" I said, "Who?" Mama said, "The Queen of the Waters." From that time on she would tell me stories about the queen who would save humans.

My mama and my sister both told me that once she saves someone, they are always safe in the water. They also said that she provides all the fish and seafood and that her waters can heal and refresh. I will never forget what happened that day or the feel of being pushed up out of the water. I guess she saved me for a purpose, and I am very grateful.

If you feel drawn to the Queen of the Waters, then you can set up a small space for her. You can add things to the altar that you feel should be placed there. On my altar I have a bowl filled with rocks and river water. I also have seashells, because she is over all waterways. The altar is your own personal space, and there are no set rules for decorating it. I do give her a nice bottle of perfume; it seems to help with the work.

Fishhook Drawing Work

I am going to give you a small drawing work that can be done for any type of drawing. You need a blue candle, fishing line, and a fishhook. On your altar, place a photo of whatever it is you need around a blue candle. Say your prayer and petition, then light the candle. On the other end of the altar "hook" the photo or petition to the fishhook and tie the fishing line on the hook. Every day say your prayers and petition, and as you are saying them, pull the hook a little closer to the candle. You continue this until the hook is right next to the candle. Once that first candle burns out, if your petition hasn't been granted, then you repeat the process until you have what you were petitioning for.

When your petition has been answered, remove the photo or petition from the hook, then burn it to ash and blow it to the east. Keep the fishhook and work with it when you need to draw something into your life.

Saint Anthony of Padua

Feast Day June 13th

Saint Anthony, like Saint Peter, is a road-opening saint. He also sits by the door, and he is the finder of things that are lost. I sometimes work with St. Peter and St. Anthony at the same time. I petition St. Peter to open the roads, and then I petition St. Anthony to go find whatever it is I need to either help myself or my client. St. Peter sits on the left side of the door, and St. Anthony sits on the right side. If you look at St. Anthony's attributes, you will get an idea of what to offer him: you can offer him red wine as it represents the blood of Jesus, white lilies as he is often pictured holding them, of course the baby Jesus as he loves him dearly, and the flaming heart. These can be pictures you have printed out, prayer cards, or statues. Books also have a special place with St. Anthony. Back in his day books were hard to come by, and he valued them. Most folks burn brown or white candles when petitioning St. Anthony.

Folks know that he is wonderful at finding things that are lost or misplaced, but he will help with much more than that. The symbol of a heart on fire is very dear to St. Anthony; for this reason I burn red candles to him when there is any issue going on where the heart is concerned. He can be petitioned to help with all matters of the heart, be it healing or other matters such as love. If you are separated from your love, you can petition St. Anthony to draw them back.

Lost Love Drawing Work

Set up a small altar with a deep red cloth. You need some lilies, red wine, a photo of you and your lost love, and a red candle. Lay out the cloth and set out the lilies, the candle, and the wine in a triangle setup. Place the candle at the top, the wine to the right, and the lilies to the left. With a red permanent marker draw a red heart around the photo. Place the photo in the center of the triangle, light the candle, and call on St. Anthony, petitioning him to bring your love back to you. Continue to pray over the altar daily until the candle burns out. If you still haven't heard anything, keep the work going until you do.

Personal Power Drawing Work

St. Anthony is also great to petition when it comes to low self-esteem and personal power. The heart is a powerful organ and a lot of the time it rules our head, and sometimes we get pulled down. If your personal power is low and sometimes you just wish you could hide, this work may help you. You need a deep red cloth for the altar, a red bowl, a photo of yourself, a red candle, some lovage (*Levisticum officinale*), and some dark red wine. Place the cloth on the altar and place the bowl in the center of the altar. Place your photo in the bowl, then the red candle, then sprinkle the lovage around the candle and cover the photo and the lovage with the red wine. Knock three times, call on St. Anthony, and light the candle. Pray your petition over the work as long as the candle is burning. I'm not gonna tell you how to pray the petition because this type of work is very personal and should be between you and St. Anthony.

The Seven Holy Spirits

The Seven Holy Spirits are found in the Bible in Isaiah 11 V 2. These seven spirits can be prayed over any work or target whose spirit is weak and low. These are the seven spirits that God has gifted each one of us with. The problem is that when we are growing up into adults, sometimes things happen that weaken our gifts. If you feel you have lost one or more of these spirits, then you can dress a white stick candle with holy oil and pray the Isaiah 11 V 2 over the candle, then you call out each of the gifts. Do this work for seven days.

I would like to clarify what I mean by "lost a spirit." If you find yourself always making the wrong choices and always not understanding why this happens and keeps happening, then I would suggest that you do the work and petition for the spirits of wisdom and understanding to become stronger within your spirit.

It is also possible that the gift of wisdom is missing from your spirit; you miss the wisdom you need to make the right choices or to follow the right path in your life. The last one is the power of might. Many folks become weak in spirit and do not have the wisdom or the understanding of how to get their personal power back. Then this causes folks to make the wrong choices in their life because they don't have the power to do anything else. Sometimes these things happen in childhood but they also happen in adulthood when a person is beaten and brought down by life. Do the work and get your personal power back, because with a strong personal power comes all the tools you need to succeed in life. You are the only person who can hold you back; anything else and you are giving away your personal power to a person, place, or thing!

Isaiah 11 V 2

2 And the spirit of the LORD shall rest upon him, the spirit of wisdom and understanding, the spirit of counsel and might, the spirit of knowledge and of the fear of the LORD.

So the Seven Holy Spirits are:

1. The Spirit of the Lord
2. The Spirit of Wisdom
3. The Spirit of Understanding
4. The Spirit of Counsel
5. The Spirit of Might
6. The Spirit of Knowledge
7. The Spirit of Fear of the Lord

PLACES OF POWER

IN CONJURE WORK, there are many places of power where the worker can go to petition the spirit of place to help them. Let's discuss the most well known first.

THE GRAVEYARD

Over the years, as Conjure has been plastered all over the internet, graveyard work has been glorified. Many have been led to believe that they can just run willy-nilly through the graveyard calling on any spirit that is there and it is safe. They have been led to believe that petitioning someone who is unknown to them is safe.

I'm here to tell you that it is *not* safe, and I'm gonna tell you why. My mama used to tell us, "The dead can't hurt you, but they can make you hurt yourself." I often pondered those words growing up, and to be honest, I never really understood what she was talking about until I got online.

Everyone is responsible for their own actions and the work they will or will not do; if things go wrong, they have no one to blame but themselves. You should use caution when you are working with any spirit, but you really need to use caution if you are gonna be working with graveyard spirits. Always use your common sense when doing this type of work.

Before I go further into this, I want to make something very clear: this is my opinion and how I have been taught to interact with the dead. I am by no means saying it is the only way or the right way, but it is my way, the way I feel safest doing the work. I'm not saying anyone is wrong; I am simply going to give you the reason why I don't work with spirits in the graveyard that I don't know.

Here is an example. Many seek to work with unknown soldiers, because they are believed to know how to follow orders. I can't disagree with this, because it is true that soldiers are trained to follow orders and to do what they are told to do in time of war. But let's think about this for a minute:

* How many of these soldiers really hated being told what to do?
* How many of them ended up with some type of mental illness?
* How many of them were put in the position of doing jobs that they could never talk about?

All these questions potentially add up to trouble. If you are petitioning an uncontrollable soldier spirit, how do you know what type of spirit you are calling up?

My brother was a marine. I will never call on him to help in any situation because I know what his mental state was; I know the issues he had in life. Just because someone has passed doesn't automatically turn them into a saint or a new person. I was taught that it is dangerous to go to the graveyard and rouse up spirits you don't know, folks you didn't know in life, unless it is your blood kin and sometimes not even then depending on how they lived. Just use your common sense when you are dealing with the graveyard and the dead that live there.

I understand that sometimes we live far away from where our dead are buried. So what do we do in those cases? Should one never do graveyard work at all if they can't get to the grave of a family member? Of course not! There is always a way around any issue. Southern folks are known for taking care of their family members' graves. On holidays the graves are decorated. They are kept clean and prayed over. I visit my dead kin often. But if you live away from your dead kin, you can always adopt a grave. I'm sure some of you are wondering what in the world I mean by "adopt a grave." You can go to a graveyard near you and find a grave that needs tending. Sometimes you will get lucky and the grave will speak to you; other times it might take a little work, but in the long run it will benefit you and the spirit.

To prepare to go to the graveyard on your hunt for a grave to adopt, you need to make sure you are well protected. Here are the steps I take for going to the graveyard. I take a spiritual bath with a wash made of bay leaf, baking soda, and four table-spoons of salt; once the wash is cool, I pour it in my bathtub. The whole time you are in the bathtub you should be praying for protection and guidance. Under the soles of your shoes you need to place a bay leaf and a pinch of sulfur in both shoes. You need to gather the items you need to bring with you. On this trip you need a pendulum that works well with you—meaning one you work with and have had great success with getting the answers you are looking for—a gallon of water, a rag, some type of spiritual water, and a small spray bottle with a mixture of a capful of ammonia, four tablespoons of salt, and a pinch of sulfur added to the water—mix the ingredients well.

Before I move on, I want to give a little more detailed instruction about the spiritual water you need to bring to the graveyard to clean the headstone with. There are many commercial spiritual waters on the market today like Florida Water and other premade waters. Florida Water isn't a traditional conjure water, although a lot of folks work with it. If possible, you should always try to make your own products; they will always be more powerful than any premade product you can buy because you know what has gone into the product and you will be the one praying over your product. I'm gonna give you two recipes for the wash to clean the headstone with. One recipe will be all items you probably have in your pantry; the other one will be a mix of pantry items and items you might need to buy at a conjure shop. Each of the washes will have three ingredients in them to represent the Holy Trinity.

Wash One

3 Bay leaves

Basil

3 Tablespoons of salt

Wash Two

Frankincense

Myrrh

Rue

Place the roots and herbs into a gallon of water in a pot on the stove. As the water is heating and beginning to boil, pray Psalm 23 over the wash. Bring the water to a strong boil, then turn off the fire and cover the wash to steep. Once the water is cool, pour the water back into the gallon jug. Once you have everything ready, then you can find a graveyard that calls to you.

I don't usually write full instructions on how to do graveyard work, but I figured I might as well give safe instruction because tons of folks who don't have a clue of what they are doing are just going into the graveyard trying to work. As a teacher and a writer, I feel better by trying to share safe information for working with the dead than letting the reader guess at what I am trying to say. If you have to work with non-blood kin, then you should take every step you can to get to know the spirit you will be working with and let them get to know you. There are a lot of unkept graves in graveyards all over the country, so I'm pretty sure you won't have a hard time finding an unattended grave in your area. When I go to the graveyard, I pray all the way there; prayer is important because it offers protection from unwanted spirits trying to cling to you when you enter and leave the graveyard.

When you reach the gate of the graveyard, you need to drop some change as you go over the threshhold of the driveway; different folks will tell you different amounts to drop. I drop at least five coins going in, and remember, you have to have coins to drop when you leave. You pay to get in and you pay to get out.

You may have to go more than once if you don't find a grave where the spirit is willing to work with you. Forcing a spirit is never a good idea because they can turn on you. But different folks work with Spirit in their own way, and I am by no means saying my way is the right way or the only way. But it is the way I was taught and the way I have worked all these years.

Say a prayer to your ancestors and ask them to protect you and ask them to help you find the right person for you to adopt and honor. You should get out of the car with the pendulum already in your hand; just stand there for a few minutes and listen to get the feel of the place. If you feel weird or feel scared, then simply get back in the car and drive out of the graveyard; remember to pay at the gate when you leave. Drive up the road a little ways, get your spray bottle, and spray the bottom of your feet and around your body while praying Psalm 23. Then get back in the car and go home to try again another day.

But if everything feels peaceful, then it is time to get to work. You need to be relaxed and listen to your inner voice—you know, that lil voice we all have that guides us? Look around and see if you can see a grave that looks like it hasn't been visited in a long time. When you find one, walk over to it holding your pendulum and in a calm, normal voice ask if you can say some prayers for them and clean off the grave.

You might get lucky at the first grave you approach, but if you don't, then try another grave. This may take awhile, or you might not have any luck at the graveyard you picked. You may have to find another graveyard altogether. If you are lucky and find a grave, then you need to clean the grave off, wash the headstone with your wash, and say some prayers for the person who rests there. This is gonna take awhile; you have to build a relationship with the spirit. You can't just jump in with both feet. Take your time and do it right, and you will benefit from your kindness. Go weekly and bring flowers, maybe a little candy, and say some prayers for them. When you need them, they will be there for you.

When you are ready to leave, pay your way out by dropping your change at the gate, then drive away from the graveyard until you are away from the gate. Then get out of the car and spray the bottom of your feet and around your body with your spray. Then get back in the car and head home. Try to go visit the grave at least once a week for a few months. You will begin to feel a shift in the feel of the visits; a bond will grow between you and the spirit of the grave you are tending. If there ever comes a time when you need graveyard dirt, you should first ask permission. Even though you will be paying for the dirt, you should never just take it without asking. That is disrespectful.

Graveyard dirt is worked with for many different reasons. It is worked with for protection, love, crossing, and domination work, just to name a few. Over the years of being in the online conjure community, I have heard folks say many "dos and don'ts" about collecting graveyard dirt. Some say there are certain times to go to the graveyard, certain phases of the moon, what days one should collect dirt on—the list goes on and on. I go anytime I need to petition the spirits for help. I'm not going to wait until the full moon or whatever if I have a job that needs to be done. The only rule I do follow—and this is my own rule—is that I won't petition help from spirits who are not my kin or I didn't know in life.

Why?, you ask. Because I am not going to ask some unknown spirit to help me. To do so is very foolish and very dangerous. You should only petition spirits you have a bond with; use your common sense. If you are going to petition an unknown spirit, then you need to introduce yourself to them, clean their grave, and get to know them before you jump in with both feet. Just because a person has passed on doesn't mean that all of a sudden he or she has become a good person.

There are only two things that I stand firm on, and I think everyone should do them before and after going to collect dirt or doing work in the graveyard.

* First, focus on your personal protection: take a good protection bath before you go to the graveyard, and wear

or carry a good protection amulet on your person while you're there.

* Second, cleanse and make sure you come home alone: before you get too far down the road from the graveyard, you need to do a light spray cleansing, and when you arrive at home after your trip, you need to do a really good cleansing.

Let me explain to you why I follow these two rules. Spirits roam the graveyard; that is where they live. Not all of them are happy about being dead. Some of them can be very nasty. Also when you go there, you will be building energy with your prayers or whatever you plan to do. Entities are drawn to this energy that you are putting out. Why in the world would you go there without protection? Please use your common sense. Now you've done your work and you go home. Maybe nothing attached itself to you, or maybe it did. Why take the chance? Cleanse yourself just to be on the safe side. It's better to be safe than sorry.

Here are the steps I take on a normal trip to the graveyard. They have served me well. When I get to the road that leads to the graveyard, I leave an offering. I call to the spirit Keeper of the Gate and ask permission to enter. By the time I reach the gate, I know whether I can go in or not. You may be thinking, *how do I know?* Well, we as humans have a built-in alarm system; if I feel fear or nervousness, then I am by no means going to proceed.

At the gate, I leave another offering. I usually just drop some change or I leave three pennies for the Trinity. I can't stress enough how important it is to be respectful when you enter the graveyard. You are there to ask for assistance. "Ask" is the key word here.

When I reach the grave, the first thing I do is say a prayer for them. Then I will talk to them for a while. Even though I will be paying for the work or dirt, no one likes to feel used, not even the spirits. When I feel the time is right, I will tell them what I need help with. At this point it is important that you listen. Why? Well, there have been a few times when I was led to do something different than what I planned on doing. Not only did the work turn out right, but also it was very powerful.

When I'm ready to get my dirt, I use my pendulum to find out where is the best place to get dirt from. I always check myself. I have learned over the years that this is a good habit to have. Sometimes I will get dirt from more than one place on the grave. It just depends on what the pendulum says.

Here's a work to drive away someone who is causing trouble. Make a dollie, then add a pinch of hotfoot powder along with any personal items you may have of the target's and the ashes from the petition. Then you need a little graveyard dirt; it doesn't take a lot of dirt to get the work done. The dirt should be taken from the foot of the grave, and you should petition the spirit to move the target out of the way and to hold them down so they can't come back. I always just take a tablespoon or so. Once I get the dirt, I'll drop some coins in the hole where I take the dirt. This pays for the dirt.

I usually work with my mama. I never give whiskey; she was against any type of alcohol. So I always bring her strong black coffee. I will either place a cup in the hole and fill it with coffee or just pour the coffee in the hole. She smoked Pall Mall cigarettes, so I always bring her some. I will open the pack and light one. I give her three puffs then place the cigarette on the edge of the hole so she can smoke some. I leave the rest of the pack for her.

Once I give all the offerings, I will give thanks for the help given. I do give my daddy whiskey every once in a while. The thing is you don't want a drunk spirit on your hands, so be mindful of the offerings you give. When the work is done, I head home.

When I am at the gate, I also thank the gatekeeper for letting me in and for protecting me. I leave more change on my way out. By leaving more change at the gate, I know the gatekeeper won't let anything follow me. Once I drive out of the gate, I don't look in my mirrors until I am well away from the graveyard. I don't want to maybe draw a spirit to me that may be lingering outside the graveyard. Always be respectful of the spirits, and always pay your debt to them. You really never know when you may need them.

We need to remember that graveyard work is a lot more than just enemy work. We also need to remember that when you go to the graveyard, it is important that you protect yourself. I have found that some folks have been taught or believe that they can go to the graveyard and do work without protection. This is a misconception. Before you go to the graveyard, you need to do a protection work for yourself. Common sense tells us this; you are entering the place where spirits live.

When you finish your work at the graveyard, you also need to cleanse yourself. You don't want to take a chance that something might have followed you home. I always carry a spray bottle with me that has one bottle capful of ammonia, table salt, and frankincense added to the water. I spray my feet and my body with this spray after leaving the graveyard while saying the Lord's Prayer. Once I get home, I do a good cleansing. It's always better to use caution when doing this type of work.

THE CROSSROADS

The crossroads is the next powerful place I want to talk about. What is a crossroads? A crossroads is a place where one road crosses another or where more than one road meets. In the ole days before paved highways, there were plenty of dirt roads that crossed or even three roads that met; but nowadays all city roads are paved, and it is getting hard to find dirt roads in some rural areas. Working with the crossroads in Conjure is very powerful work. The crossroads can either be opened or closed for a target. It's important that you understand the difference between works that open the roads and works that close the roads. I'm gonna try to explain and give a few good examples of works and why one might need to do them.

First, I need to say this before I go any further: just because you know how to do a work doesn't mean you have to do it. I also want to remind y'all that every action causes a reaction, and this work should always only be done if it is justified. If the target has the knowledge and knows how to do reversal work, then you could get hit with your own work if it was unjust. Don't let the simplicity of this work fool ya; it is very powerful and should never be done in anger! Also you should remember that any work that is done can be undone if the target knows what they are doing and you alone are responsible for the work you do.

What exactly does it mean to close someone's roads? It basically means to block them, to stop them from moving forward in life. The crossroads can be worked with to stop promotions, to stop judgments in court, to stop slander, to stop an enemy from moving against you, the list goes on and on. I want to give one more bit of caution here: once you do the work, it is out of your hands and there is no turning back and no stopping the work. It is in the hands of Spirit once it is done, so always be mindful of the works you do. They are your responsibility alone.

Back in the day, very few folks owned cars, so there wasn't as much traffic on the roads as there is today and it was easy to get dirt from the center of the crossroads. As times have changed, workers have had to adapt to the changes, so now unless I can find a dirt crossroads, I take dirt from the corners of the crossroads.

I have been known to wait until the wee hours of the morning when most folks are sleeping to take my broom and dustpan to the center of the crossroads on a dry road before the dew falls and sweep some dust up, but most of the time I take it from the corners.

There may come a time when you feel it is justified to stop someone for whatever reason. You can do this work by taking their photo or name—the photo works better—and burying it under a stop sign at a crossroads. You need to call on the spirit of the crossroads and say your prayers and petition that the target be stopped as every vehicle is stopped at the stop sign. To make the work last, you can add to your petition by saying something like "May so-and-so be unable to move until the stop sign is moved!" This will lock the work down.

I was taught that the crossroads represents the numbers four or five. Four is represented by the four corners of the crossroads and the number five comes from the four corners and the spirit that sits in the center of the crossroads. Some folks say that spirit is the devil. I believe it is St. Peter and he holds the keys to the pearly gates of heaven, which are all the roads.

Container Work

This work is gonna be done by using a container to hold the target and a set of five candles to be burnt to do the work. I like using tealights for this type of work because they don't make a mess and the little tins get hot which in turn heats up the work. A small glass jar is used to hold the work. For this lil work you are gonna need a photo of the target, two nails, a lemon, red pepper, four toothpicks, a small glass jar, dirt from the four corners of the crossroads, and five tealights.

1. Using a pencil that has no eraser, draw an X over each of the target's eyes and three X's across their mouth.

2. Petition St. Peter to stop the target from whatever they are doing to cause trouble.

3. Now take the two nails, flip the photo upside down, and run one nail through the photo going downwards. Run the other nail left to right through the photo. This is called "nailing a target down."

4. Cut the lemon in half, sprinkle red pepper on each side, and petition St. Peter to make the target's mouth burn, as if on fire, if they even breathe your name.

5. Place the photo between the two pieces of lemon.

6. Use the toothpicks to hold the lemon pieces together.

7. Place the lemon in the jar and cover it with more red pepper and add the crossroads dirt.

8. Seal the jar.

Once the jar is closed, you should never open it again. Shake the jar and call the target's name. Pray your petition after each calling; you will do this three times. This is called "working the jar."

Having done this, you are ready to place your candles in the setup. The setup is the way you lay the candles out over the work. This is very important because you can actually cross yourself up if you try to do a road-opening work for yourself and set the candles out in the wrong layout. You are going to lay the candles out top, bottom, left, to right; meaning you are going to "cross" over the jar to lay the right candle down. Then the fifth candle goes on top of the jar. You light the candles in the same way you laid them out.

As the candles are burning, you need to repeat your prayers and petition at least three times over the burn. Then the next day you repeat the whole process of working the jar again. Keep working the jar until you see your results. Once you have achieved positive results—the desired outcome—you can either keep the jar or you can throw it away in running water.

This work may seem harsh to some, but Conjure is not all sugary sweet! You have to remember that this work was birthed out of slavery—survival was of upmost importance. The protection and survival of self and family came first above all else. You never know when you may need a heavy hand if you or your family is threatened.

Road-Opening Work

Now that the heavy-handed work is out of the way, it's time for some road-opening work. This type of work is to help remove blocks.

Sometimes our money gets funny: it seems there is more going out than is coming in. Calling on St. Peter and doing a road-opening work usually helps get the money flowing again.

St. Peter sits behind the door. In the ole days folks would just tack his picture up behind the door. Nowadays it's easy to get a statue of him if you want one, but the picture behind the door works just as well as the statue. If you don't have a statue of St. Peter and you are having money issues, don't spend money buying a statue; just go online and print out a picture of him and tack it behind the door. For this work you need a can, a bright yellow candle, dirt from the four corners of your house, dirt from the four corners of a crossroads, three tablespoons of sugar that you have named each one "God the Father, God the Son, and God the Holy Spirit," and some change from your pocket. Pray over each of the ingredients and then add them to the can. Make sure you are petitioning St. Peter as you are saying your prayers to ask him to remove all blocks from your life and to open the roads for money and prosperity to enter your home.

Remember you don't have to have money to be prosperous, so make sure you add both money and prosperity to your prayer and petition. Once you have the can "loaded"—meaning that all the ingredients have been added—then you need to pray over your candle, before placing the candle in the can and lighting it. It is important to pray over the work daily, and place the can behind the door for St. Peter to work. You can keep this work going to keep a flow of money coming into the home.

Conjure Bags and Packets

Conjure bags and packets are one of my favorite works; they remind me of my grandma. She would always tie her money up in a handkerchief and put it in her bosom. I always thought she was so cool. She had what she called a "hand bag," but you only saw her carry it to church or town. The rest of the time she kept a little money in her apron pocket and the rest was in the "girls" as my granddaughters call them. In honor of my grandma I'm gonna tell you how to make a handkerchief packet. They are easy to make and small enough to carry.

Before I talk about the packet, there are just a couple of things I need to tell you first. These are very important to the success of the work no matter what you are working on.

* When you are making a packet and you are trying to draw something towards you, then you always fold the handkerchief or material towards you.

* If you are trying to remove something, then you will always fold away from yourself.

I'll talk more about this further in the book. It is really important you remember this because you could cross up your money by folding the handkerchief away from you for a money packet. I don't want y'all to say, "Well, Starr said . . ." Nope she didn't. You will find places where I repeat these instructions because they really are important.

For the packet you need a new white handkerchief and dirt from the crossroads (you can either take the dirt from all four corners or you can just get the dirt from one corner). You also need a small rock from a bank. The day before you make your packet set the rock in a tealight setup and call on the spirit of banking to fill the rock with the power to pull in prosperity. You need a photo of yourself that you have burned to ash, a small magnet to draw, and four coins from your wallet. You need four tealights for the setup to set the packet in once you have finished.

1. Lay the handkerchief out flat on the table and then fold it in half bringing it towards you.

2. Run your hand over it a few times to get a crease so you will know where to place your ingredients. Just a small reminder: you should be praying your petition the whole time.

3. Now load your ingredients into the hankie. Pick up each ingredient and hold it up close to your mouth, say your prayer and petition over each one of the ingredients,

then place it in the center of the hankie on the crease line. Adjust the ingredients so they are kind of piled on top of each other.

4. Once you have them in place, you need to feed them before you wrap them up in the hankie. When I say "feed," I mean to put a little oil on them or a little whiskey.

5. Now fold the hankie in half, making sure your ingredients stay in place. This is the tricky part. Make sure you are praying your petition the whole time you are working.

6. Now catch each side of the hankie as close to the ingredients as you can because you are gonna have to fold the hankie towards you without losing the ingredients.

7. Once you have the ingredients held tightly, then you make one roll in the hankie while saying your prayer and petition. You repeat the process until the hankie looks like a thin snake.

8. The next step is a little tricky too because you are now going to tie a knot in the hankie without letting it come unrolled or losing the ingredients. Now make a loose knot in the hankie; then you say your petition in a strong voice and at the end of the petition you pull the knot tight. You are gonna make the knots, pulling each one of them as tight as possible at the end of your petition. Once you have the knots tied, you can trim off the excess of material, cut it as close to the knot as possible without undoing the knot. Then you need to feed the packet either whiskey or spiritual oil.

9. Set the packet on the table and lay out your candles.

10. You are going to lay the candles out top, bottom, right, left and light them in that order.

11. Say your prayers and petition over the setup at least three times while the candles are burning.

12. When the candles go out, you can carry the packet either in your bosom or pocket.

You need to feed the packet once a week for the first three months and set it in a candle setup. After the three months you can start to feed it once a month and set it in the candle setup. If you keep the packet fed with your prayers, petitions, candles, and whiskey, it should work well for you and continue to work for a long time.

THE BANK

Our next place of power is the bank. There is money going in and out of there all day long. The tellers do nothing but touch money the whole time they are at work. It is like a double-edged sword because the bank can either help you or take away from you. I don't do works to cross up folks' finances nor do I teach how to do that type of work; that is what I was taught as a young worker and I still follow that rule. I do, however, believe that we should do everything possible to keep our money flowing, so we can live our lives the way we want to.

You can do a lot with that little envelope they put your money in at the bank. Just think about it for a minute: those lil envelopes have been sitting in that bank around all that money. They are picking up the spirit of money and prosperity. You can burn those envelopes into ash and add the ash to your prosperity and money works. Here's a money oil recipe you can make yourself to add power to all your money workings.

Money Oil

You will need base oil—this can be any oil you have on hand—plus a bank envelope, a small magnet, a pinch of gumbo filé, shredded money, a pinch of cinnamon. Burn the envelope to ash while praying over it as it burns. Then add it to your oil base. Next add each one of the other ingredients as you pray over them. Once you have all the ingredients added, pray the Psalm 23 into the bottle; then close the lid on the bottle and place the bottle in a cross setup of tealights. Let the tealights burn out and repeat the setup and prayer process for five days. Then the oil is ready to work with. You can use the oil to dress yourself, candles, doors, windows, check stubs, and anything else you can think of to draw money into your home.

THE POLICE STATION

The police station is a very powerful place: folks are locked in and they are let out. This type of place is like a double-edged sword. The dirt can be worked with to open or close doors for folks. The dirt from the police station is worked with in all just judge works and law stay away works. So for those who don't know what just judge and law stay away works are, I am gonna try to explain it so you will be able to do a work if you had to.

Just judge works go along with court case works, which of course are needed if you have to go to court for some reason. You will want the court to see you in a favorable position. This is where the just judge work comes in. I was taught to sweeten the judge so my clients will be seen in a good light and have a successful outcome. One way to do this is to have a bowl of sugar and burn your candle in the bowl. To the bowl of sugar you need to add a photo or the name of the judge, devil's bit, and some Master of the Woods. Then you need to burn a purple candle and pray to St. Peter for justice; petition him to make sure the judge is just and fair with you. You can also place the judge's name or photo in the bottom of your shoe facing downward so you are walking on them. You need to keep the work going until court is over. Then you can leave it at the crossroads for St. Peter.

I want to share the prayer that I pray over my works when I am doing just judge works. It's a prayer that I have prayed over many of court case works over the years. It is the revised prayer from the just judge candles. I rewrote it so it would have a better flow when I pray it over my work.

Just Judge Prayer

Oh, Divine and Righteous Judge, you who created the earth. The King of Kings!

My Blessed Lord, defend my interests from that of all adversaries, guide me, protect me, and defend me at all times.

Holy Father, make my life fulfilling and righteous without rash and reckless decisions, protect me from dangerous paths, cruel prisons, treacherous rivers, all enemies, demonic possessions, thieves, being referred to negatively, being the victim of false testimony. Free me from those that would bind me and chain me, never allow my conquering or that of my soul, never may I be within the reach of their eyes (be seen), feet (be located), hands (be apprehended).

As my ONLY Judge, I pray, Father, please protect me from their words, their spears, swords, knives, firearms, or any means by which to mortally injure me. You alone are my Judge, blessed Father. Hide me from those who try to bind me in that sacred sore at the Divine's side, and cover me with the sacred blood of Jesus so I will be protected from injury, death, imprisonment, captivity, and never within reach of the hands of any enemies; may my enemies be overcome/conquered.

May the Holy Father free me, the Holy Son keep me, the Holy Spirit
accompany and speak for me.

In the name of God the Father, God the Son, and God the Holy Spirit
by the power of the three I am free! Amen.

The law stay away work is needed in all cases where you are
dealing with the law. There are times when folks are just law
magnets; every time they turn around they are getting a ticket
or being stopped or having to go to court for some reason or
another. There are two different works I like to do for clients
and loved ones who are having these types of issues. I'm gonna
share them both with you. I usually do them both at the same
time, but you could only do one if you feel that is all that is
needed.

Law Stay Away Work One

For the first work you need an orange candle, a new rosary, a
bowl, some dirt from a courthouse, and dirt from a stop sign
near your home. Place the dirts into the bowl and wrap the
rosary around the candle. Tap the candle on the table three
times and then call St. Peter. Petition St. Peter to put a stop
to the harassment and to protect you from the law; petition
him to fill the rosary with his power of protection and to let
your roads be open without hindrance from the law. Place the
candle in the bowl and light it. Try to go at least three times a
day and pray your petition to St. Peter. When the candle burns
out, take the rosary and hang it in your vehicle.

Law Stay Away Work Two

The next work is to make a conjure bag to either carry or place
in your vehicle. You need to sew a small red flannel bag. This
should be about three inches tall and about two and a half

inches wide. Use blue thread to sew the bag up with; on each stitch pray your petition to St. Peter. Make three knots at the end of the sewing when you are ready to tie off the bag. Name one for God the Father, God the Son, and God the Holy Spirit. You need a Southern John root, dirt from the four corners of a crossroads, dirt from the courthouse, olive leaves named after God the Father, God the Son, and God the Holy Spirit, and a pinch of devil's bit.

Add all the ingredients into your bag and then hold the bag open next to your lips and blow three breaths into the bag. Then you say your prayer and petition to St. Peter. Then you tie the bag off using some of the blue thread: cut a length of the blue thread and wrap it around the top of the bag, then you tie three knots in the name of God the Father, God the Son, and God the Holy Spirit.

You need to feed the bag a little whiskey or law stay away oil. Then you place the bag in a candle setup. Keep working the bag in the setup for at least five days, going daily to pray your petition over the bag. When the bag is ready, you can either carry it on you or you can place it in your vehicle. You will need to feed the bag either whiskey or law stay away oil once a week to keep the bag strong. Once a month you need to place it in a candle setup to keep the power of the bag working.

The Church

The church is another powerful place to draw blessings. Those buildings hold the power of thousands of prayers said in them; the power of the elders who have prayed there weekly, if not daily. For peaceful home work you need to get the dirt from the four corners of the church. For those who might not know what "peaceful home" work is, it is a set of works within conjure to draw forth peace in the home when there is a lot of fussing, fighting, and turmoil going on. The work is done to stop whatever issues are going on in the home and to bring peace to all those living in the home.

Along with the dirt from the four corners of the church, you also need dirt from the four corners of your yard. If you live in an apartment building, then get the dirt from around the building as best you can. Mix the dirts in a bowl with a cup of sugar and a pinch of lavender—lavender brings forth relaxation and will help settle folks down. As you are mixing the ingredients together, pray and petition the Holy Trinity for peace and protection of your home. The Holy Trinity is God the Father, God the Son, and God the Holy Spirit. So your prayer would go something like this: "I call on the Holy Trinity God the Father, God the Son, and God the Holy Spirit. I pray and petition you, Holy fathers, to bring peace into my home; I petition and pray that you will hobble the devil and send him packing, let peace rain down upon my home and family!"

Before I move on, let me say this: when I use the word "devil," it doesn't always mean the Christian devil. In my culture a person, place, or thing can be named a devil. Let's say I am having an issue with one of my children, I automatically say, "not today, Satan," meaning I ain't putting up with no foolishness today. Or I might say, "the devil's a liar"; this can mean that I am not claiming what is going on and I will not be dealing with any craziness. Anyone who wants to do conjure work should learn about the culture and the ancestors it comes from; this will give you a strong foundation and a good understanding of the works.

You need a blue or white glass-encased candle and some lavender oil. Dress the candle with the lavender oil and say your prayer and petition over the candle. Then walk through the house with the "unlit" candle while praying that peace reign throughout the home. Then take the candle into the kitchen, which is the heart of the home, and light it. You can also make a wash with a pinch of the mixture you have in the bowl and some lavender. Add the ingredients to a pot of water and bring the water to boil; then you cover the pot and let the wash steep. Once the wash is cooled, place it in a spray bottle and spray it through the home. Don't forget to pray over the wash as it is boiling. You can also dress the doorknobs and furniture with a little lavender oil so when the target—the one causing the issues—touches it, they will settle down.

THE HOSPITAL

The hospital is another strong place of power, although this place too could be worked with as a double-edged sword. Like with harming someone's money, I was taught to never cause an illness in someone. I am a healer first; healing work is the first works I was taught at age seventeen when my son's godfather taught me how to remove fever, nightmares, and infection by working with an egg, broom, roots, and a candle. That is the foundation my first works were built on; I have never forgotten the lessons he taught me, nor will I ever forget him and his knowledge he shared with me to help my child. Only God can heal, but if you know the right prayers and have the right tools, then you can pray and petition for the healing that is needed. Prayers are answered daily in the walls of a hospital; all those prayers build power and draw the spirits of healing.

If you have a loved one who is ill and in the hospital, if possible brush them down with an unlit white candle. Wrap the candle up in a white cloth, and bring it home with you. Get a photo of the hospital and a photo of the issue they are having. If it's the heart, then get a picture of a healthy heart, and so on. Take the photo of the heart and write their name on it while praying for healing, then burn the photo to ash and place the ash in the white candle. Place the photo of the hospital facing inward on the glass for the candle. This way the spirits of healing that roam the hospital will see that the heart is healthy. Light the candle, and say your prayers and petition over the candle daily. Keep the work going as long as it is needed.

ROCKS

Rocks are a powerful part of this work. Some of them are unmovable and this makes for some strong conjure work when you are trying to keep an enemy from moving against you. Large rock formations can be found all over the world. They represent something that is unmovable and powerful. For those who are new to the work and wondering why in the world I would be working with a rock, let me explain. Rocks are heavy and they are hard to move; this is why they are great for holding folks down if you want to stop their movements. There are many reasons for doing this type of work: someone may be harassing one of your children, someone may be cheating, and someone at work may be trying to get you fired or to get your promotion. The idea behind the work is to stop them and their movements.

This type of work is also good for court case work to hold down the other party and their lawyer. There is no limit to works that can be done with rocks. If you looked under my desk, you would find such a rock with photos under it. This is one of those works that will keep on working as long as the target is kept under the rock. If you don't continue to burn on the target, then they may stick up their ugly head now and again and try to start up their ole ways. Also this work has a softer side to it than hotfooting someone. Hotfoot work is a set of works that will literally move folks out of their homes and jobs. The problem with hotfoot is there is no control over it. The target could wander from place to place and job to job for the rest of their life if the work is done right. Hotfoot should only be worked when everything else has failed and not because someone has upset you; you need a real reason to hotfoot. Once again I feel the need to remind the reader: every action causes a reaction and you alone are responsible for the works you do.

There are two different kinds of work that can be done with a rock. One will totally hold down the target and block them, and the other one will just hold them down to keep them from moving against you. I have to warn you to remember that any work done can be undone; during a reversal work, the target may even be set free. If they are knowledgeable enough to know to do a reversal, you could also be blocked from reaching a goal. It won't last but it is possible, so just keep that in mind. Make sure your work is justified and you are not just doing it because you don't like someone or they made you upset.

Work to Hold Someone Down

If you ever have an issue with someone and you just want to stop them and what they are doing, then you need a pencil with no eraser on it, their photo, and a heavy rock.

1. Take the pencil and place three crosses over their eyes, ears, and mouth. You do this so they won't be able to see you, hear you, or talk about you. Sometimes I will do what is known as a double action work. A double action work is a work that has two works done to the target. So for example, I will run a set of needles or rusty nails through the photo, starting from the top of the head downward and then across left to right.

2. Once you are done with the photo, place it on the floor facing upward and put the rock on top of it.

3. Set a tealight on top of the rock and say your prayer and petition over the work.

4. Repeat the process until your target has stopped whatever they were doing.

5. If you feel the work has served its purpose, then you can let them go by simply undoing the work and burning the photo to ash. Then you face the east and blow the ashes away from you with a prayer for the target to go in peace.

Work to Hold and Block Someone

If you want to do a more heavy-handed work, then you place the photo facing the floor upside down and place the rock on top of it. This not only holds the target down, but it also blocks the target's movements. This is a good work to do in court cases or situations when you and the target are trying to get the same job at work. This type of work holds down the competition. This is also a great work if you have a supervisor who just will not stop trying to get you fired or who is trying to stop you from getting the promotion you deserve. Don't let the simplicity of this work stop you from achieving your goals in life. Do the work and reap the success.

THE HOME

Your home is another spot that has powerful places in it that draw in or remove, and you have access to them 24/7. I want to touch on a few of them: the doors, windows, the stove, and the bathroom. The ole folks say the windows are the doors to our souls; I don't know about that, but I do know that the windows of our homes are a way for Conjure to come through. Since I was a small child, I remember my mama having mirrors in the windows. The mirrors act as a boomerang, so if work is sent towards your home, the mirror will deflect the work back to where it came. The shiny side of the mirror—the one you look into—should be placed looking outward from all the windows in the home facing the road. They don't have to be large mirrors; just small makeup mirrors will work. When you bring them home from the store, all you have to do is run them through some cool running water in the sink and let them air-dry. Once they are dry, pray over them and place them in the windows that face a road. Rinse them once a month after that to keep them fresh.

The doors to your home are the entryways into your home; they are like a portal and should always be protected and cleansed. You should wash and cleanse your front and back doors at least once a month. By now everyone reading this book will know how to make a wash and what a wash is; so make a cleansing wash with four tablespoons salt, a cap of ammonia, and a pinch of borax. Then you clean your doors with the wash. Clean the outside first and then clean the inside of the door. You also need to dress the doors on both sides with holy oil or some kind of spiritual oil once they are clean. You also need some kind of protection by your door where folks enter into your home. A broom is a good tool to have by the door; it can be worked with to sweep folks in or to sweep them out of the home.

If there are folks that come to your home and you don't want them to return, then that's an easy fix.

1. Once they cross the threshold of the door on their way out, throw salt behind them.

2. Using your broom, sweep the salt all the way to the road, while praying they don't come back.

3. Sweep until you have it in the middle of the road, then turn around and go back to the house.

4. Before you enter your home, brush yourself off with the broom; then go on in the house and put the broom back behind the door.

5. You can place the broom head up if you prefer not to have folks coming in and out of your home, or you can place it head down to sweep in all the company you want.

The stove is also a place of power. The flame from the burner draws in spirit just like a candle does when you say your prayers and petitions over it. I have a copper pot I keep on the stove over a low flame. I like to keep it going to draw good things into my home, and it makes the house smell really good. I place three cinnamon sticks named after the Holy Trinity, some shredded money, a magnet, and some dried orange peel for attraction going in the pot. This also makes a good spray to spray on your door stoop and your doors to draw in prosperity. You can also add some of the wash to your mop water to keep prosperity coming into the home.

If there is a lot of stress in the home, then you can place lavender, the plant devil's shoestring (*Viburnum* species), and three tablespoons of salt named after the Holy Trinity in your pot. Keep it going over a low flame; say your prayer and petition the Holy Trinity to let peace rain down upon your home.

The last room I want to talk about may shock you, but in the ole days many folks were dumped in the outhouse to run them off and get them out of the way. Their photo might have been used, but most of the time their foot track was picked up and dumped in the outhouse. The yards in the ole days in the rural areas were sand or dirt, so it was easy to pick up someone's footprint in the sand. Yes, I am talking about the bathroom, the toilet as a matter of fact. There is an old work where you write the target's name on a piece of toilet paper, then you wipe your behind with the paper and flush it down the toilet. This work is done to not only turn their life upside down but to also put them in the crapper and move them away from you.

Another way to use the toilet in your work is to burn the target's photo to ash and flush the ashes down the toilet. When you flush, the toilet will take them away from you and they will end up in the sewer. I also have jar works sitting behind my toilet so every time the toilet is flushed my target feels it. They have been there for years.

As you can see, there are many places of power that you can work with to help you in your work. I have only touched on a few of them. This is by no means a complete list, but it is my hope that you now have some new information on places that can help add power to your work. I'm not saying my way is the right way or the only way, but it is how I was taught to work with these powerful places. The only thing stopping you from success is you. Do the work and draw in the success you are looking for and need in your life!

LIGHTS

I WANT TO TALK about candles and oil lamps in this section of the book. I believe I have a few tricks to share that you may not know about.

Working with candles or what some old workers call "lights" or "vigils" is very old in Conjure, but what is even older is the oil lamp. Oil lamps date back to before the time of Christ. Fire has always been a part of spiritual work from the time the first people discovered it. Whether through candle lights, lamps, or an actual fire, folks and spiritual workers alike recognized the power of fire and what you can do with it.

The flame of a lamp or candle burning draws Spirit. They are both great tools to draw Spirit into your work. Let's look at the benefits of candles in the work; then we will look at the benefits of working with oil lamps. I feel that both are very beneficial to the work in their own way.

CANDLES

I have found in my workings that wax acts like a magnet and will hold your prayers or anything that you are trying to remove, and as the candle burns, your prayers are sent out. I was taught there is one rule that one needs to follow if you want your work to be a success, and that is before you do any type of candle work, you need to give yourself a good cleansing. You can do a quick cleansing using a small stick candle, a small broom, or a chicken foot. You simply brush yourself going downward while praying to the Holy Trinity that everything be removed that is not good for you or that could hinder your work. Once you do the cleansing and dress your head and hands with some type of oil, then you are ready to start your work. This may seem like a lot of effort just to light a candle, but it is the little things that can make or break a job.

I take extra steps with my works because I don't want to have to redo works over and over. I feel if I put a little extra into my work from the start it will be a success. The first thing I do when I am going to start a new candle work is of course a quick cleansing, then I wipe the candle down with a wash I make to clean my candles with before I put them to work. This cleans off anything that the wax might have picked up in the making of the candle or from folks handling the candle in the store.

You need three tablespoons of salt, three bay leaves, and a pinch of rue. Pray over each ingredient, and then add it to your pot of water. Bring the ingredients to a boil and remember to pray over them. Once the mixture comes to a boil, turn the fire off and let the wash cool. Once the wash is cooled, use a white cloth and wipe the candles that you will be working with off. Make sure to wipe the inside wax that is in a glass-encased candle off too. Let them air-dry before you light them.

Then I wake the candle up; I stir up the spirit in the wax by blowing three breaths into the wax and tapping the candle on the altar three times. This will get things moving so you can fix the candle to do the job you need done. I load a little of my ingredients into my candles by either using an ole screwdriver to make three holes in the wax of a glass-encased candle or a hole in the bottle of a pillar candle. If you can't make the hole, then you can set the candle in a bowl and sprinkle the ingredients around the candle. Any of these methods will work. Once you have the candle fixed, you need to call Spirit into the candle; call the Holy Trinity first and then whatever spirit you will be working with. It may seem like a lot of work, but once you get into the habit of it, then the steps will become natural. There are different types of candles you can work with like stick candles, vigils, pillars, jar candles, and pull-outs.

If you want to draw something to you, then you roll your candle in the ingredients *towards* you while praying your prayer and your petition. To draw and sweeten, you can use magnetic sand (sand that has been magnetized), powdered sugar, the herb Master of the Woods, and cinnamon. To remove someone or something from you, roll the candle *away* from you; the ingredients for removing are a photo or petition burned to ash, calamus root, red pepper, and a dirt dauber nest. Oil the candle well with some kind of spiritual oil, and then you roll the candle away from you while saying in the name of the Holy Trinity that the person or situation is removed from you and state your petition and prayer in a strong, firm voice. I was taught to work with stick candles for this type of work although nowadays there are a variety of candles to choose from.

I think one of my favorite candles other than the stick candle is the pull-out candle. They are good for candle burning because you can mark the candle before you load it into the jar and then feed the jar that will contain your candle with powders, roots, herbs, photos, and so much more.

It is also easy with a vigil candle—a candle that is encased in glass and usually burns about six days—because you can read the wax as the candle burns and find signs in the glass as the smoke rises from the wick. Here are a few ways to tell what is going on with the burn as the candle flame does the work. If the vigil burns black in the flame or in the glass, then you need to do an uncrossing on yourself and redo the work because there are blocks standing in your way. If the flame is small or keeps going out, then there are blocks in your work or someone is trying to stop you from getting what you want. If the flame is strong, then that's a good sign your work will be a success. You can read these signs in any candle you burn including oil lamps. You simply have to understand the way the flame works. If you watch the flame as the candle burns, you'll get an idea of where your work is headed because the candle flame will always tell you how the work is going and what actions might need to be taken.

Remember that prayer plays a big part in successful candle burning. So does faith. When you work, you have to know with all your heart that the job is a success. There can be no room for doubt; otherwise you might cross your own hard work and efforts up! Below you will find a few simple candle works using a stick candle, a vigil light, and a pillar candle.

To Draw Money

This is a simple little work to draw money into the home. You will be working with a stick candle to draw in prosperity. You need a white handkerchief, powdered herbs, your petition, cinnamon, sugar, and some type of spiritual oil. Lay the white handkerchief out on the altar. Then burn your petition to ash and mix with powdered herbs, or you can use just cinnamon and sugar if that is all you have. Write your name on the candle, then dress the candle towards you with oil (from top to bottom). Roll the candle in your powder towards you on the white handkerchief. Holding the candle close to your mouth, say your prayer, then light your stick candle and place it in a candleholder on the white hankie. When the candle burns out, bury any leftover wax in your yard at the East with the hankie wrapped around it.

Loaded Blockbuster Candle

There are many times when nothing we do seems to work. When those times arise, it is time for some blockbuster work to remove whatever is in the way holding us back. In this work you will use a large pillar candle. If you can find an orange or purple candle, then use one of those colors, if you can't, then use a white one. Purple is a powerful color and also one of the colors mentioned in the Bible, so it is a good color to work with for this work. Take a pair of small scissors or a knife and dig a hole either in the bottom or the side of the candle. The reason you use scissors or a knife is because you are removing the blocks that are holding you back. Scissors and knives cut away things, so they will cut away any magic that has been done to block you. Save the wax from the hole. You need a bowl to sit your candle on. You need John 14 V 1–14 torn from an old Bible or copied; then you write your petition on top of it. You also need one small piece of High John root. Burn the Bible verses to ash along with your petition; mix this with a little powdered angelica root. Load your powder and the High John into the hole. Fill the hole with the wax you removed. Write your name on the candle along with "I knocked and the door was opened." Set the candle on the plate and sprinkle the leftover powder around the candle. Light the candle and pray all blocks be removed. Take any leftover wax to the crossroads along with five pennies and leave it there.

JOHN 14 V 1–14

1 LET NOT YOUR HEART BE TROUBLED: YE BELIEVE IN GOD, BELIEVE ALSO IN ME.

2 IN MY FATHER'S HOUSE ARE MANY MANSIONS: IF IT WERE NOT SO, I WOULD HAVE TOLD YOU. I GO TO PREPARE A PLACE FOR YOU.

3 AND IF I GO AND PREPARE A PLACE FOR YOU, I WILL COME AGAIN, AND RECEIVE YOU UNTO MYSELF; THAT WHERE I AM, THERE YE MAY BE ALSO.

4 AND WHITHER I GO YE KNOW, AND THE WAY YE KNOW.

5 THOMAS SAITH UNTO HIM, LORD, WE KNOW NOT WHITHER THOU GOEST; AND HOW CAN WE KNOW THE WAY?

6 JESUS SAITH UNTO HIM, I AM THE WAY, THE TRUTH, AND THE LIFE: NO MAN COMETH UNTO THE FATHER, BUT BY ME.

7 IF YE HAD KNOWN ME, YE SHOULD HAVE KNOWN MY FATHER ALSO: AND FROM HENCEFORTH YE KNOW HIM, AND HAVE SEEN HIM.

8 PHILIP SAITH UNTO HIM, LORD, SHOW US THE FATHER, AND IT SUFFICETH US.

9 JESUS SAITH UNTO HIM, HAVE I BEEN SO LONG TIME WITH YOU, AND YET HAST THOU NOT KNOWN ME, PHILIP? HE THAT HATH SEEN ME HATH SEEN THE FATHER; AND HOW SAYEST THOU THEN, SHOW US THE FATHER?

10 BELIEVEST THOU NOT THAT I AM IN THE FATHER, AND THE FATHER IN ME? THE WORDS THAT I SPEAK UNTO YOU I SPEAK NOT OF MYSELF: BUT THE FATHER THAT DWELLETH IN ME, HE DOETH THE WORKS.

11 BELIEVE ME THAT I AM IN THE FATHER, AND THE FATHER IN ME: OR ELSE BELIEVE ME FOR THE VERY WORKS' SAKE.

12 Verily, verily, I say unto you, He that believeth on me, the works that I do shall he do also; and greater works than these shall he do; because I go unto my Father.

13 And whatsoever ye shall ask in my name, that will I do, that the Father may be glorified in the Son.

14 If ye shall ask any thing in my name, I will do it.

Attraction Vigil

Sometimes there is need for a work to draw something to us that we need or want. This could be a new job, a place to live, a promotion, or even a new car. There is an ole saying that nothing is free in life and you have to work for what you want. I have found that the best way to do this kind of work is to burn hard until you reach your goal. "Burning hard" means that you will keep the candle work going; before one candle burns out you should light another and keep the work hot. For this job you need a red or a white vigil. You also need a large flat magnet, a round mirror, and a white plate.

You need a picture of your desire. Write your name in the wax, as close to the glass wall as you can. Around the wick write "the Lord is my Shepherd, I shall not want." Make four holes in the wax, top, bottom, right to left. Load the vigil with your petition and a pinch of attraction powder along with a few drops of oil. Tape your picture to the outside of the candle, so the picture will be looking at the flame as the candle burns. Set the mirror on the white plate, then set the magnet on top of the mirror. Set your candle on the magnet. Pour a ring of sugar around the candle. Then pour a ring of whiskey over the sugar. Light the candle and say your prayers that what you are in need of will come to you. Let your candle burn until it burns out but make sure you have your new candle burning before this one goes out. Keep it hot! Then you should bury any leftovers in your yard facing east or by your front door. If there is wax left in the jar, I dig it out and that is what I bury.

OIL LAMPS

Now I'll move on to oil lamps, one of my favorite ways to burn. In the ole days most folks used oil lamps to light their homes. So it only makes sense that they would use these lamps in conjure work. I use the liquid candle oil they sell at most large craft stores, not the kerosene lamp oil; the kerosene, although it is traditional, just makes a mess. The ancestors used it, I'm sure, because that was all they had to burn the lamps with. Most wax back in that day and time was made from all sorts of fats and the waxy substance from the tallow tree. I don't think many of them could afford or get honeybee wax. When I need to do a long-term work, I prefer to use the oil lamp instead of candles. Unlike candles, as long as you keep the lamp full of oil, the flame will never be extinguished until you choose to turn the flame off.

In some ways, the oil lamp is safer to use than candles. For one thing you don't have to worry about the jar breaking or the candle not burning right because you added too many ingredients to it. You also have less chance of the ingredients catching on fire because they are held in the base of the lamp with the lamp oil and the fire never gets near them. I know in days gone by people stopped using this type of lamp because the kerosene smokes so bad and has a bad odor. The liquid candle oil doesn't have an odor nor does it smoke when being burnt. The other good thing about working with a lamp is the ingredients are infused into the oil, which makes the work stronger. Everyone has their own way of working. This is just another way to get a job done.

The first thing you need to do is find you a lamp that you like. Once you have your lamp, you need to make up the wash to cleanse the lamp before you began to work with it. Make sure not to get the cotton wick wet, because it will take it days to dry, but the good thing about the cotton wick is that cotton absorbs so it will pick up the power of the prayers, petitions, and ingredients you add to the bowl of the lamp. Let the lamp air-dry. When you are ready to load the base of your lamp, you need some kind of white cloth laid out to place your roots and herbs on as you pray over each one of them. Sometimes I will tie them up in the cloth and place the bundle in the base of the lamp. This keeps them from making a mess when I need to change them out.

Just like when you are working with a candle, each ingredient has to have your prayer and petition said over them before they are added to the lamp base or bundle. Once you have everything together, you then need to pray over the base again before you add the oil. Your wick should be turned down on a low flame once you have everything loaded. If it seems like the wick doesn't want to stay lit, then use a sharp pair of scissors to trim it with. Cut a pinch off of it and try to light it again. Below you will find a couple of different works that will help you. They are long-term works that you can keep going as long as there is a need for them.

Love Thyself Lamp

The first lamp I want to offer is what I call a "love thyself" lamp. Oftentimes in our busy lives we let ourselves go because we are so busy taking care of others. Sometimes we feel like we are beat down or just lost, and yet we always manage to keep pushing and doing for others. Do something for yourself and make this lamp. The first thing you need to do is some strong cleansing baths; you need to take at least three of them. It's important to remove all the buildup from doing for others and just living before you start your lamp. I bought a new lamp for this work, but you can use whatever you have at home. You need a small white piece of cloth and some red cotton thread. You need some lovage root. (This was one of the first roots I was taught to work with. Lovage promotes love and self-love.) You need a photo of yourself after the cleansing work. You need Jezebel root if you are a woman and a High John root if you are a man. Each of these roots promotes self-power in women and men. You need a pinch of bloodroot for the ancestors, you need a magnet to draw, and you need a pinch of calamus to give you the upper hand.

Pray over each of the ingredients and lay them on the white cloth. Burn your photo to ash, then add the ash to the cloth. Gather the corners of the cloth and wrap the red thread around the top of the bundle. Then you make three knots and on each knot you call out your petition. Then you need to feed the bundle with a little whiskey or some spiritual oil. Then you need to set the bundle in a setup of four tealights. Pray over the bundle at least three times while the candles are burning.

I'm sure you have noticed that I haven't told you what to pray throughout the whole making of the bundle and the empowering of the bundle in the candle setup. That is because this is a very personal work and you alone know what it is you need in your life to draw back your self-love and self-worth. When the tealights burn out, then you can add the bundle to the base of the lamp, pray your prayer and petition into the base, and then fill the base with the lamp oil. Light the wick and keep the lamp going with the wick turned down low. Make sure you say your prayer and petitions over the lamp daily.

Road-Opening Lamp

I want to also share a "road-opening" lamp that can be worked to keep your roads opened. You need your lamp, and you need dirt from the four corners of the crossroads, as well as dirt from the four corners of your property. You need to print out a photo of St. Peter on the cross that you will burn to ash, a key, and you will need some shredded money. You can also add any roots or curios you would like to the lamp. This is just a basic lamp. You need to call on the Holy Trinity and then call on St. Peter. Petition them to remove all blocks out of the roads that are holding you back. Petition them to protect your home and your prosperity. Then set all the ingredients in a cross setup. Once the candles go out, place all the ingredients into the base of the lamp. Even St. Peter's photo is added in with the other ingredients. Fill the base with the oil and light the wick. Adjust the flame on the wick to a low flame. You should say your prayers and petition over the lamp at least three times a day.

Domination Lamp

The work below is for a domination lamp. Sometimes situations call for heavy-handedness. Use your own judgment.

There are times when a heavy hand is needed. I know some folks will never do this kind of work because they feel it is somehow wrong, but you have to remember conjure workers don't have a lot of rules and regulation that they have to follow as long as the work is justified. We are all responsible for the actions we take, so always make sure you have justice on your side before you jump in with both feet. I call this a domination lamp, but it also controls the person it is being worked on and adds a little confusion. A dirt dauber nest is used to control, dominate, and confuse a person. A pinch of red pepper will also confuse a person, but I add it to this lamp to give the lamp a little heat. Take my advice when I say a pinch: I mean just a pinch. Master root is used just as the name implies so that you will be the master. High John conquers all things that stand in your way. Calamus root dominates, controls, and defeats a person's will.

You need to get the target's sock. Remove a small piece of cloth from the heel of the sock. It needs to be a dirty sock. If you can't get a sock, then just leave it out of the lamp. You also need to make a small wax dollie and place a few pieces of calamus root in the head of the dollie. Name the dollie for the target. Then you need to write out your name paper. For this you will write the person's name inside of a circle nine times. Once you have everything ready, make a bed of the herbs inside the lamp; then place the heel of their sock, the name paper, and the dollie on top of the herbs. Use the rest of the herbs to cover up the dollie.

When you get the base of the lamp loaded, pour your oil in slowly so you won't disturb the bed. If this lamp is being worked on someone you love, add a little lovage and a little powdered sugar to the herbs. This will sweeten up the person. Not everyone who uses this type of work does so just to dominate another person. Sometimes this type of work is the only solution they have. Like my mama used to tell us, "You don't know what goes on behind closed doors."

In some cases leaving and moving on may not be an option. So people do what they have to do.

Say your prayers and then light the lamp. Work the lamp daily for at least the first seven days, then once a week after that. Use your common sense and always remember anything that can be done can be undone. If your target is smart enough to do reversal work and you have been unjust in your workings, then look out 'cause you're gonna get hit.

CONJURE WATERS

IN CONJURE WATER IS a strong part of the works. I am not talking about premade waters that are bottled and sold in stores. These waters are collected by the worker and made into washes and baths as needed or added to a work when it is called for. A lot of new workers are not taught to work with the natural waters that are everywhere in nature.

The elders didn't have the time or, more important, the money to spend on store-bought waters. They didn't even have running water in their homes; they had to tote water from the well into the house. Even in my lifetime I have had to prime the well pump in order to get water to bring in the house for cooking. Into the seventies, some rural areas in the Deep South didn't have running water and were still having to use slop jars and outhouses. You need to study the past to understand how the work came about; most folks nowadays can't get their minds around the way it used to be in the rural South.

I've written about these waters before in other books, but I am going to go into more detail here. This is a big part of the work that I feel is being lost as folks who don't know how to work with natural waters are leaving it out of teachings and filling the void with store-bought waters. It is very important that this work not be lost or whitewashed with ingredients that the ancestors had no way of getting, much less working with.

BLUE WATER

Blue water is made by adding bluing (also known as laundry blue) to river water. You petition the spirits of the river to help you see what you need to see when you are doing divination. Blue water is also good for protection washes and sprinkles or to dip herbs in during cleansings to be brushed down on the client or whomever you are doing a cleansing on.

Fresh waters can also be worked with in the same manner. Fresh waters are well water, springwater, rainwater, and creek water. They are all used in spirit workings and also to refresh the spirit of one's work.

CHAMBER LYE

I know there are some workers who like to use their own urine in works. My issue is that urine sours when it is closed up. So what happens when the urine in the work goes bad? I would think that whatever work had been done would go bad also. I mean, my common sense tells me this would happen. I do understand the concept of it, but I don't think it was meant to be closed up. The idea is just like an animal marks their spot: one's own urine can be worked with to nail down a property and such. In this instance I do believe it would work and work well, but I don't advise anyone to lock their urine up in a bottle or a jar. Let me say this: I have heard about witch's bottles containing the witch's urine for protection; someone in a class I gave once pointed this out to me. This is what I said and I stand by it: "I can only speak from a conjurer's point of view. I am not saying anyone is wrong, only that it is not conjure work and that's all I know."

DISHWATER

If there was a lot of arguing in our home, my mama would work the dishwater to bring peace. So dishwater is worked with for a peaceful home. If there is fussing and fighting in the home, then after supper wash the dishes in a dishpan and throw the water out the front door of the home.

HOLY WATER

Water that has been blessed by the church can be worked with for protection, healings, and adding power to your conjure work. Some workers make their own holy water, but I'm sure it holds the same power as the water made in the church if we believe in the power of places. Most Catholic churches will let you get holy water if you ask for it.

HURRICANE WATER

Hurricane water is exactly that: water that was collected during a hurricane. It is worked with to stir things up just like a hurricane. This type of water can be worked with to stir up an enemy's life or to turn their world upside down. When working with this type of water, please remember that justification is the key. If you throw at someone just because you don't like them, that work can be reversed if they know what they are doing—just a bit of a warning.

RIVER WATER

Water from a river can be used for all types of removal work. You do the work, and then you throw the work in the river, where the current takes the issue away from you as the tide goes out. This is a simple but powerful way to remove something or someone from your life.

STAGNATED WATER

This is any type of water that is not moving. It can be found in the swamps, ponds, and also stumps. It is worked with when you are trying to stop the target or if the work is being done for bindings, confusion, crossing, and enemy work. After this type of work you need to do some cleansing work to make sure you don't have any residue on you. Stump water can be used in the same way; only stump water and the spirits of the tree can also help with all manner of healing works.

STORM WATER

This type of water is worked with to stir things up, just like a storm does. It works great when things have been building and coming to a head. Lightning water is worked with in the same way and is also used for crossing work, healing, and for stirring things up. Be careful because you might heat up the work too much.

TAR WATER

Tar water is used for protection and uncrossing as well as the reverse. Back in the day it was easy to get tar because tar was used to pave the roads and the workers would share a little with you. Today it is hard to find, but you can get Creolina, which is a commercial brand sold in some ole feed stores. Creolina is made with a base of coal tar and sold as a deodorant cleaner for the home. It can be used to spiritually clean the inside and the outside of the house. I have written about this before, but I think it is important to share again as the ole ways are being lost.

You need to be careful with Creolina because it will burn you if you get it on your skin, but it works. Just a capful in a mop bucket or in a spray bottle can be used to cleanse the house. If you mop your house, make sure you clean the corners. Once you have mopped the whole house, take the leftover mop water and pour it at the end of your walkway in a straight line. This will put a straight line of protection across your walkway; if anything or anyone tries to cause you issues, they have to cross that spiritual line.

Creolina mixed with a little holy water and salt can offer an added protection to your yard. Make a bucket up and dress the four corners of the yard and around the house. Creolina will also kill any tricks that have been thrown in your yard. You can also wash your door, stoop, and sidewalk down once a week to bring in blessings. Make sure you only work with it in a water base.

TOILET WATER

This is good for all types of work where you are trying to remove someone or something from your life because you just flush them away from you. It is also good for enemy work when a heavy hand is needed for justice.

WAR WATER

War water is a work that was thrown against an enemy's door. In this day and age if you tried it, you might go to jail. As times change, we must adapt to these changes. War water is used in a campaign to start a war against another person. Today that would definitely not be a very good idea, but you can use the same technique—just in a different way. I understand the reasoning of busting the jar against the door: glass cuts, not only that but there is a violent element of throwing the jar at the door.

But it is the ingredients in the water that make the water work. Instead of busting a jar, you can use the war water as a sprinkle, by laying a trick on the person you have a conflict with. You need to collect some storm water. To the storm water you need to add some rusted nails, some broken glass, rose thorns because they prick and make you bleed, needles, and dirt where three dogs had fought in a yard. You also need to get some dirt or a rock from the target's yard or driveway. While you have the war water setting up, you need to go daily and shake the container while you pray your prayer and petition over the container. You need to go at least three times a day and work the jar, making your petition and prayer for the purpose of the water.

Let the water sit until it becomes stagnant, then it is ready for you to drop somewhere the target will get in it by walking through it. You can adapt anything to make it work without changing the meaning of the work. Don't get yourself in trouble trying to follow an old way of doing things when you can just do the work a little differently and have the same effect. Make sure you take a cleansing bath after dropping the water for the target. You don't want to cross your own self up. Always be mindful.

DIRTS & DUST

IN THE OLE DAYS DIRT was collected from many different places. The dirt that was collected was mixed with powdered herbs and that mixture became a powder. Dirts are a large part of Conjure, although it seems that the new age conjure workers don't work with them as much as workers have in days gone by. It seems that the only dirt most folk work with is either grave-yard dirt or dirts dealing with the law. There are many more dirts out there for a variety of conditions. If you are interested in this work and you want to make the products the ole way, then you are gonna have to go out and collect the ingredi-ents you need. In days gone by everything was collected; there wasn't any money to buy a store-bought product.

Today most of the time workers don't work with dirts as the ancestors did. What most new age workers don't realize is that the dirts were used to make dusting powders; they are the base of real conjure dusting powders. That is why I named this sec-tion of the book "Dirts & Dust" because the dirts are used to make conjure powders. Today folks use a powder base such as talc, cornstarch, or some other powder base, and then they add color to it and call it powders for such and such. I have written about using rice powder as a base powder because that seems to be what the mainstream conjure workers know how to work with, but I decided for this book I would share with folks how I make powders. It's time for folks to get back to the basics of the work. I am sharing information that I haven't written about and have only shared with my hands-on students in the past. Throughout this section I'll share little recipes and works so you can began to make your own powders.

As I said, the base of all conjure powders is dirt from powerful places along with powdered herbs and ashes from either scripture or photos mixed in. You have to remember that in the ole days the yards were not all grassy knolls; most were nothing more than dirt that turned to mud when it rained. It was easy back then to dust someone's yard or door stoop because the powder just blended in with the yard. That is also why most folks swept their yard once a week on Saturdays—to make sure that anything that was dropped was burned in the burn pile. Another note to remember is folks didn't go visiting like they do now. They didn't have time; they were too busy working and looking after their families.

Before I move on to the dirts and recipes, I feel like I need to remind folks that this work is not all sugary and sweet. The ancestors were fighting for their lives so some of the works are hard works, but you have to remember that these works came out of "slavery." The elders were trying to survive and take care of their families. I would also remind you, the reader, that just because you "know" how to do a work doesn't mean you have to do the work; that is totally up you.

PEACEFUL HOME WORK

Here is a peaceful home conjure work I would like to share with you. It seems like there are times in the home when peace just can't be found. This is a good work to help draw peace in. For this work you will need a white vigil, a white bowl, a pinch of dirt from the front and back of your home, and a pinch each of devil's bit, three olive leaves that you have named God the Father, God the Son, and God the Holy Spirit, Master of the Woods, angelica root and some Karo syrup. Dress your candle and pray your petition over the candle, and then you need to pray Philippians 4 V 6 into the candle. Then you need to either copy Philippians 4 V 6 or tear it out of the Bible, and then you wrap it around the candle. Some folks have an issue with tearing a page out of the Bible; I don't because that is the way I was taught. You can always just copy the verse. It's the words that hold the power. Like I've said before and I'm sure I will say it many times over, conjure workers are a different kind of Christian. You should always do what feels right for you.

PHILIPPIANS 4 V 6

6 BE ANXIOUS FOR NOTHING, BUT IN EVERYTHING BY PRAYER AND SUPPLICATION, WITH THANKSGIVING, LET YOUR REQUESTS BE MADE KNOWN TO GOD.

Place your white candle in the bowl, then light it. Sprinkle your roots and herbs around the vigil, then pour the Karo syrup over the other ingredients. Set a cross setup around the bowl using tealights. Pray over your candle setup daily while calling out each person's name that lives in the house. Peace will rain down on your home like a light and clean spring shower.

BASIC TEALIGHT SETUP

To keep from repeating myself over and over, I'm gonna give the instructions on the basic tealight setup for working the powder to get them ready. Each setup will contain five tealights. You light the tealights the way you lay them down. To open the roads, you set the tealights top to bottom down right to left

and the fifth tealight sits on top of the powder. To lock someone down or close their roads, you set the tealights down top
to bottom left to right and then the fifth one sits on top of the
powder.

Dirts & Dust Used in Conjure

BANK DIRT: used for all money works and financial secu-
rity. Here is a recipe you can work with to dust your money
to draw more money into your home. You need some dirt
from a bank, your photo burned to ash, and you need some
powdered bayberry root and the dirt from the four corners
of your home.

CHURCH DIRT: used for blessings, healings, and protection work. It helps in repairing broken relationships
as well. You need some dirt from a churchyard, dirt from
a crossroads, powdered olive leaves, and powdered bay
leaves. Mix them together in the name of the Holy Trinity
and then place them in the basic candle setup.

COURTHOUSE DIRT: used for justice and court case
work. To make the basic court case powder, you need
powdered Dixie John root, dirt from a courthouse, and
crossroads dirt. Mix them together in the name of the Holy
Trinity, and then place them in the basic candle setup.

CROSSROADS DIRT: used for opening or closing roads
in conjure work.

DIRT DAUBER NEST: worked with in all domination
work, but the dust is also good in enemy work. It adds extra
power to all work.

DIRT FROM FIGHTING DOGS' YARD: This dirt is worked with to cause the target confusion and to cause fighting and destruction.

FIRE ANT DIRT: worked with to draw or remove something or to stir things up and heat them up.

GRAVEYARD DIRT: used for a variety of conjure works, blessing or cursing.

GUNPOWDER: Although not technically a dirt or dust, gunpowder can be used in similar fashion. It's used to heat up the work and provide quick activation—an explosion of power. Also used in blockbuster work. Blockbuster powder is made with dirt from a crossroads, a pinch of gunpowder, powdered angelica root, and powdered lightning-struck wood. Mix them together in the name of the Holy Trinity, and then place them in the basic candle setup.

HOSPITAL DIRT: used for all healing works. You need dirt from a hospital, dirt from a church, dirt from a crossroads, powdered heal-all, and powdered life everlasting herb. Mix them together in the name of the Holy Trinity, and then place them in the basic candle setup.

POLICE STATION DIRT: used for all justice work and can also go into all law stay away works. To make law stay away powder, you need some powdered devil's bit, some powdered Dixie John root, and some dirt from the police station. Mix them together in the name of the Holy Trinity and then place them in the basic candle setup.

RAILROAD TRACK DIRT: This dirt can be worked with to draw or send away. Move away powder is made with dirt from a railroad track, crossroads dirt, dirt from an ant pile, and some powdered red pepper. Mix them together in the name of the Holy Trinity, and then place them in the basic candle setup.

RED BRICK DUST: is used for protection. Mix with other dirts and powdered herbs, then sprinkle across doorways and around the yard for blessing and keeping enemies out.

RIVER DIRT: can be worked for cleansing, making a dollie, or bogging a target down.

TERMITE DIRT: to tear down an enemy's foundation, to strip away their personal power. Revenge powder can be made with termite dirt, dirt from a stop sign, red pepper, and gunpowder. Mix them together in the name of the Holy Trinity, and then place them in the basic candle setup.

SALT: Biblical powerhouse of spiritual blessing and cleansing. The Covenant of Salt guarantees our blessings, preservation, and protection under God. Don't forget what happened to Lot's wife.

SALTPETER: Used in uncrossing works and to tie a man's nature.

SNAKE DIRT: If you are lucky enough to find a snake crossing, scoop up as much dirt as possible. You can work with the dirt for wisdom, protection, knowledge, and enemy works. You can make wisdom powder using snake dirt, powdered Solomon's seal root, and powdered bay leaves. Mix them together in the name of the Holy Trinity, and then place them in the basic candle setup.

SULFUR: Used for enemy work, hotfoot powders, as well as crossing conjure, sulfur can be placed in the home to drive out unwanted spirits.

TERMITE DIRT: to tear down an enemy's foundation, to strip away their personal power. Revenge powder can be made with termite dirt, dirt from a stop sign, red pepper, and gunpowder. Mix them together in the name of the Holy Trinity, and then place them in the basic candle setup.

ROOTS, HERBS & TREES

I WANTED TO DO a small section on some of the roots and herbs that are worked with in Conjure, but I also wanted to give a list of trees and the powers they hold. This is by no means a full list, but it is a basic list that you can put some good recipes together with. I don't think there is much being taught about the trees in conjure work, and you have to understand the ancestors worked with everything in nature and each tree has its own power. So this is another area where the knowledge is being lost as elders pass on. Once the knowledge is gone, it will be lost. It is important that it be shared and the work passed on.

BASE OIL

Q. What is base oil?

A. Base oil is any type of oil you add your roots and herbs into to make spiritual oil.

Here is a small list of oils that can be base oils:

Castor oil

Coconut oil

Jojoba oil

Olive oil

Sassafras oil

Sunflower oil

Sweet oil

Herbs and Roots to Use in Conjure

AGRIMONY: one of my favorite herbs. Agrimony can be worked with for protection, breaking up cross conditions, and all better business and prosperity works.

Protection Recipe

You need a small piece of red flannel and a pinch of each of the herbs agrimony, angelica root, rue, bay leaves, and the olive leaf. Pray over each herb, then add it to the flannel. And then you gather the corners of the flannel, and you tie a piece of red cotton string around the packet to hold it together. Feed the packet a little olive oil or whiskey, and carry the packet in your bosom or pocket.

ALFALFA: one of my favorite herbs to work with in all manner of money works. Alfalfa is also good when you are trying to protect your business or your money.

Money Oil

You need a pinch of alfalfa, orange peel, devil's bit, a little shredded money, and dirt from your front and back door stoop. Add the ingredients to some type of base oil; make sure you pray over each of the ingredients before you add it to the oil. Then set the oil in a cross tealight setup for twenty-one days. Make sure you pray over the setup daily as the candles are burning. Once the twenty-one days are up, you will have a good money oil to work with.

ALKANET ROOT: worked with for all kinds of money works from good fortunes to good business. To make a red fast luck oil add a pinch of alkanet root, orange peel, five finger grass—naming each herb after the Holy Trinity as you add them—to the bottle of oil. Alkanet is added God the Father, orange peel added God the Son, five finger grass added God the Holy Spirit. Pray your petition into the bottle of oil. Place the bottle in a cross setup for three days, and then it is ready to work with.

ALL-HEAL: worked with for all-around healing and to keep sickness away. All-heal can be placed in a white handkerchief with three bay leaves named after the Trinity, and the dirt from the front and back door of the house. Place all the ingredients in the center of the white handkerchief and call on the Trinity to drive away all illnesses from the folks in the house and from the house. Gather the hankie from corner to corner and make a knot, then gather the other two corners and make another knot. Feed the packet some whiskey and then place it either under the sickbed or beside the sickbed. After the person gets well, bury the packet to the west.

ALLSPICE: another great herb for money drawing and better business. You can make a floor sweep out of this herb. You need allspice, shredded money, and angelica root. Mix all your ingredients together while praying that your money be protected and drawn into your home or business.

Then add the mixture to a base oil of your choosing. Set the oil in a cross setup for three days; you will then have a good business oil.

ALUM: a bitter herb that is worked with to stop gossip, but also to remove crossed conditions. Add alum and red pepper to a bottle of oil, and say your prayer and petition over the oil. You then need to bury the bottle of oil in the west for three days. Wrap the bottle in red flannel before you bury it. On the third day as the sun is going down, dig the oil bottle up. You now have powerful stop gossip oil.

ANGELICA, or the Holy Ghost root as some call it: worked with in all protection work. It is also powerful when one is dealing with family matters and unruly children. Ole folks say that angelica root is the root of the angels. They say that this root is a strong, powerful healing root. They say that when the root is petitioned for healing, it destroys anything that was sent to make the person ill. This is a root that everyone should keep on hand.

ANISE SEED: well known for use in psychic vision oils and also the ability to ward off the evil eye. Get a base oil, and to the oil add anise seeds, angelica root, and three bay leaves. Call on the Holy Trinity for protection as you add each herb to the oil. Place the oil in a candle setup for seven days, praying over the oil daily.

BALM OF GILEAD: a biblical herb. It is said to heal hurt feelings and a broken heart. It is good when you are trying to do a cut and clear.

BASIL: worked for all money matters. Basil is also good for sending evil away. Basil is also good for protection; get a bundle of fresh basil and hang it inside your front door.

BAY LEAF: A wash of lavender, bay leaf, basil, and cinnamon can be made to wash down all the doors in the home and to clean the stoop off. This will offer a peaceful home that is well protected and draws in prosperity.

BAYBERRY: worked with for all money drawing and prosperity workings. I like to add a pinch of bayberry to all my better business and money works.

BLACKBERRY LEAVES: worked with for all reversal work. Blackberry leaves will also return the evil back to the sender.

BLACK PEPPER: Black pepper will remove fussing and fighting in a home.

BLUE FLAG: Blue flag adds extra power and protection to conjure work. It is also good for all money works.

BLOODROOT: for all types of work dealing with the family.

BROOM STRAWS: worked for protection and cleansing. The ole folks say that they will sweep away evil and witches.

BUCKEYE NUT: It is said to be very lucky when carried in one's pocket.

CALAMUS: worked with for all domination work.

CALENDULA FLOWERS: used to make a salve. It is very good for achy muscles.

CATNIP: a good herb to add to any follow me boy work.

CAYENNE PEPPER: worked with in all hotfoot work and all enemy work. It is also worked with when you need to heat a workup. You need to be careful when working with cayenne pepper because it is so hot.

CELERY SEED: added to psychic vision oil.

CHAMOMILE FLOWERS (MANZANILLA): worked with for uncrossing and protection. It is also good for nightmares. It is very good when made into a tea to sooth a nervous stomach or a restless spirit.

CHIA SEED: Mix a pinch of chia seeds with red pepper and alum to shut the backbiters up.

CINNAMON: one of the herbs that are added to the recipe of holy oil that comes right out of the Bible.

CLOVES: well known for the power that they bring to all conjure works for prosperity and better business.

CORIANDER SEEDS: good for keeping passion in a relationship and to keep your mate faithful.

CUMIN SEED: use comes right out of the Bible. These seeds are worked with when you need to deflect evil and cut away bad luck.

DAMIANA: the number one love herb. Most workers like to work with it for all types of love works.

DANDELION ROOT: carry in a conjure bag along with celery seed, bay leaf, and frankincense for prosperity and protection.

DEER'S TONGUE: Deer's tongue can be added to love work. It helps insure a ring on the finger.

DEVIL POD: worked with for a strong protection against evil and any dark spirits sent to harm you by an enemy.

DEVIL'S BIT: Holds the devil down. Devil's bit is one of the main ingredients in the run devil run products.

DEVIL'S SHOESTRING: worked with in all enemy work. Devil's shoestrings are also worked in all work to nail the devil down.

DILL: a sour herb. Therefore it is worked with in all types of souring work.

DIXIE JOHN ROOT: worked with for protection and luck. It can also be worked with to keep a spouse faithful.

EUCALYPTUS: worked with in all types of cleansing work. It is also said that it will drive spirits out of the home.

EYEBRIGHT: a healing herb first and foremost. Eyebright is also worked with in conjure work to be a will to see what is hidden and also to help the worker see clearly.

FENNEL SEED: worked with to keep away all types of government folks.

FENUGREEK SEED: Momma Starr loves this stuff! It is worked for drawing money and luck into your home. Place a small bowl of it on top of the icebox to keep money flowing in.

FERN: worked with for protection, love works, and to remove crossed conditions by brushing yourself downwards with three fern leaves.

FEVERFEW: It is added to protection packets for folks who tend to always end up being harmed or hurt in accidents.

FIVE FINGER GRASS: The ole folks say that five finger grass can do anything that the five fingers on the hand can do.

FRANKINCENSE RESIN: one of the herbs of the Bible. It is said that it is a powerful herb for spiritual protection.

GARLIC: another herb right out of the Bible. It is worked with to remove all types of evil spirits. Burn garlic skins on the stove to remove crossed conditions from the home.

GINSENG ROOT: worked with in all types of money and gambling jobs. It is also said to enhance the male vigor.

GRAINS OF PARADISE: worked with for all types of protection, money, and steady work. It is also said to make wishes come true.

HIGH JOHN THE CONQUEROR: worked with in all types of blockbuster work. It is said that there is not a block in the world that this root can't get through.

HOPS: worked with for peaceful sleep and to keep nightmares away. Get a white handkerchief and a pinch of hops, a pinch of lavender, and three bay leaves named after God the Father, God the Son, and God the Holy Spirit. Place all the ingredients in the handkerchief and tie three knots in the name of the Trinity. Place the handkerchief inside the pillow. This will help you have a peaceful night's sleep.

HYSSOP: another powerful herb right out of the Bible. It is also said to add power to all types of conjure work.

IRISH MOSS: worked with to draw prosperity and also worked with for protection.

JALAPENO: worked with to heat up all types of enemy work, from shut your mouth to run devil run works.

JASMINE FLOWERS: worked with in all types of love work.

JEZEBEL ROOT: worked with for all domination work. It is also said that it gives power and self-esteem to women. This root is a woman's root and keeps the woman in total control of her life.

JOB'S TEARS: These are very powerful. The ole folks will tell you that Job's tears can be worked to make an enemy shed as many tears as Job did.

LAVENDER: worked with in peaceful home works. Lavender soothes and cools down the spirit.

LEMON LEAVES: worked with in all cut and clear work. Cut and clear work can be worked with to remove all things holding you back.

LEMONGRASS: worked with in all jinx removing and uncrossing works. It is one of the main ingredients in Van Van oil.

LICORICE ROOT: worked with in all domination workings.

LIFE EVERLASTING: It is said that this herb promotes a longer life; it can be added to all healing works.

LITTLE JOHN TO CHEW: When you join this John with the other two Johns, it is unbeatable. It is famous for court case works.

LOVAGE: wonderful when you are working on yourself. It promotes self-love and a high self-esteem.

MARJORAM: worked with to drive off those folks who would harm your family.

MASTER OF THE WOODS: worked with in all domination and commanding work.

MINT: another biblical herb. It is worked with for breaking jinxes and to run the devil off.

MOJO BEANS: worked with in all money and luck work.

MOTHERWORT: worked with in all works concerning your children.

BLACK MUSTARD SEEDS: to cause confusion and loss of concentration when a target is being worked on.

WHITE MUSTARD SEEDS: another herb from the Bible—"Job had the faith of a mustard seed." They are good to be worked with in all protection work and works of faith.

MYRRH: another herb from the Bible that is worked with for protection work.

NETTLE: worked with for uncrossing and jinx-breaking works. Nettle can also be a crossing herb because it stings.

NUTMEG: worked with in all money matters and also all dealings with prosperity work.

ORANGE PEEL: worked with in all works concerning anything that is drawing our attraction work.

OREGANO: worked with in all matters dealing with the law, whether it is law stay away or to keep troublesome folks away.

POPPY SEEDS: worked with to cause confusion and delays in all enemy works.

QUEEN ELIZABETH ROOT: worked with by women to draw power, love, and luck with the opposite sex.

ROSE PETAL: worked with in all love and romance; rose petals are also a wonderful offering for Mother Mary.

ROSEMARY: added to all works done by women because this is a woman's herb that gives the woman extra power and puts them in charge of their homes and environments.

RUE: worked with to remove all crossed conditions. It gives the worker power to help find and destroy all enemies known and unknown.

SAGE: burnt to clear out an area. It also brings forth blessings and helps with wisdom and the common sense to find the answers that one is seeking.

SARSAPARILLA ROOT: worked with for a peaceful home, prosperity, and to draw good health into the home.

SASSAFRAS ROOT: worked with for all money, prosperity, and success works. Sassafras oil is also good for the treatment of head and body lice.

SELF-HEAL: worked with in all health matters. It is said to help clans and heal the sick.

SLIPPERY ELM: worked with when you want to hide yourself and the work that you are doing from your enemy.

SOLOMON'S SEAL ROOT: named for King Solomon of the Bible. This root is for wisdom, power, and protection in all conjure works.

SPANISH MOSS: for good or evil conjure workings; can be used to protect your home or draw money; also very useful for crossing work.

SPIKENARD: another biblical herb used for love workings. Spikenard is good to add to all your love works along with a pinch of Master of the Woods.

STAR ANISE: for protection, good luck, prosperity, and healing works. It is also said to help with psychic power.

THYME: good for all money and prosperity works. It is also good for cleansing and protection works.

TOBACCO: You can work with tobacco leaf to bind and hold an enemy down. Tobacco is also good for feeding a spirit and drawing Spirit to an altar.

TONKA BEAN: good for all workings of love and luck. The ole folks say that it is really lucky if you carry three tonka beans tied up in a white handkerchief and fed whiskey once a week.

WINTERGREEN: worked with to draw prosperity, money, and good luck.

TREES

You can work with any tree in Conjure. I do feel that you need to know a little about the different types of trees. When you know their characteristics, you will find many ways to work with them. All roots, herbs, and trees are worked with for the spirit they hold inside. That spirit, when it is fed, will give your work the added power it needs to be a success.

APPLE TREE: worked with for truth, luck, and wisdom.

CEDAR WOOD: worked with for protection and also for rotting a relationship. Have you ever noticed how a cedar tree always rots from the inside out? This tree makes for some powerful conjure work.

COTTON: good to work with in protection works, defense works, and blessing works.

HOLLY TREE: well known for protection. The leaves of the tree have sharp points that can draw blood. The trees are usually planted on each side of an entrance to protect the folks inside the building. The leaves are also very protective.

HONEYSUCKLE: worked with in all types of sweetening work. The vine of the honeysuckle is good for binding lovers.

LIGHTNING-STRUCK WOOD: adds power to any type work. It works really well when doing commanding, courage, love, blockbuster, or success work.

OAK TREE: used for power and protection. It also removes crossed conditions. Oak is worked with to add personal power to any work. It is also worked with to help with cleansing works to remove jinxed and cross conditions.

OLIVE TREE: biblical tree used for blessing and protection. You can make an all-purpose dressing oil by adding olive leaves to oil. Add the leaves to any peaceful home or peaceful works.

ORANGE TREE: worked with to draw and for all attraction work.

PEACH TREE: worked with for all love and sweet works.

PINE TREE: good for healing works and for sealing things or folks off. Pine sap closes things. Pine resin is also good in healing works. It was worked with in the ole days to seal cuts and scrapes.

TOBACCO LEAF AND SUCKER: Tobacco leaves are good to wrap work in, and as the leaf dries, the work gets stronger. The sucker does just as the name implies; if it isn't removed from the plant, it will suck the life out of it.

WEEPING WILLOW: worked with to help remove cross conditions and jinxes; but also to put on cross conditions and jinxes. It is said if you bury an enemy under the willow tree, they will do nothing but weep.

TOOLS OF CONJURE

THERE ARE MANY ITEMS that a conjure worker works with. Most of them you can find around your home. I know I have touched on these in other books, but some folks that will be reading this book might not even know what conjure work is, and I want to make sure folks understand what I am talking about. I am just gonna give you a few things I work with and an idea on how to use them. This is not a full reckoning, of course; it's just a small list of things I use. But you will get the idea on how to add things you have at home to help you with your work.

The other thing I want to touch on in this section is how to write a petition. The petition is a very important part of this work. Your petition tells Spirit exactly what you are asking for. Before I write out my petition, I will sit down and think of what exactly it is I want to achieve. I may write it out a few times before I get the wording right. The most important part of writing a petition is to make sure your petition is clear and to the point—I can't stress that enough. Words are power, and Spirit listens to our prayers and petitions. I'm gonna give the same examples I always give because that is what folks mostly want: a good job and a good relationship.

PLANNING YOUR PETITION

Below is an example of what I am talking about with writing a petition. The wording is everything, and the petition should have an easy flow to it so you will be able to pray it over your works. I am by no means saying this is the only way to write a petition, but it is what I teach and how I write mine. Too many words get in the way of the flow of the prayer; you need to keep it short and to the point. Let's say I need a job, so I decide to do some work to help me find a job. If I write my petition out and state "I want a job" or "I want a job doing whatever," then I'll get just that—a job. I may hate the job and not get along with my coworkers or my boss. Also this could be a job doing anything, but what if I change the wording of the petition? Let's try the petition this way:

Date:_____ Birth_____

Name_____

I want a job doing _____ . I want to make more than enough money to make ends meet (or you can place the amount of pay you want). I want to be comfortable with my new boss and the people I work with. I want to be seen as a favorable asset to the company. I want a raise within _____ amount of time. I want this to be the perfect job for me.

Signed _____

You see from the example that you are stating exactly what it is you want from your new job. You want a job that you are good at and where you will be able to be promoted.

Here's one more example.

Let's say you want to bring a new love into your life. You're ready to find someone you can live with and be happy with. So you sit down and write out your petition: "I want someone to love me. I want him to be crazy about me. He can't live without me. I want him to worship me; he will never look at another woman." What could be wrong with a guy like this—he would be perfect right? Wrong! This guy would drive you crazy; he would suffocate the life out of you. He would be so worried about what you are doing during the day he might not even work. He may even become abusive. Why? Because he is so nuts about you.

Do you see what I am getting at? You want to draw someone who is loving, caring, and kind; someone you can find true happiness with, someone who is a good listener and will be interested in what you have to say. How about if we wrote the petition this way:

Date:_____ Birth_____

Name_____

I want a new mate brought into my life. Someone I am compatible with. Bring me someone who will be interested in what I have to say. Bring me someone who will be a good provider, who will love, honor, and cherish me. Someone who will be supportive in whatever I may choose to do. Bring me someone I can live my life out with in peace and happiness.

Signed _____

Do you see the differences in the two petitions? One would draw someone who would never let you have peace of mind and would suck the life out of you, and with the other you get everything you could want in a partner and much more.

There is no rush to get the petition down. Take your time because this prayer will be a large part of what Spirit will listen to when you say your prayers. Watch the words you use when you are writing out the petition. Spirit will not try to decipher what you mean; they will take your words as a fact. They will believe this is what you want to draw into your life. You don't want the spirits to be confused when they are trying to help you succeed in your work. Your higher power will bring you what you are asking for; it doesn't matter if it is good for you or not.

Before you sit down to write a petition for any type of work, I suggest doing one cleansing to clear your mind so you can think straight and be clear in your meaning of what it is you need. It may seem like a lot of work, but the benefits are well worth the effort. You have to remember our higher power will try to bring us what we ask for. I want you to think before you write out your petition. By doing so, you won't get something you didn't mean to ask for. Some folks just pray their petition over their work and don't stick with the same petition every time. That may work well for them, but I have found repetition builds power. Not only does it build up power over the work, it also lets Spirit know nothing has changed and you are still waiting for your results. You need to keep any confusion out of the petition and be clear and on point with your prayers.

HOUSEHOLD TOOLS

There are many useful tools around your home that you might not even realize are there. It is important to remember that the ancestors were held captive as slaves. They had no money to buy things they needed, so they made do with what they could find or were given. That is why this work uses things that most folks already have in their homes and at hand. You don't need to get a bunch of expensive store-bought items to get the job done. A lot of household cleaners were used in work because they had access to them. Most of these cleaners are from the early 1900s and can still be bought today. Since cleansing work makes up a large part of this work and a very important part, if you have a condition on you or have just blocked yourself with your attitude towards life, then these items will be able to help you get things moving around again. I think folks fail to understand that the way we think and the way we speak about our lives tell Spirit, "Hey, this is what I am claiming!" Remember repetition is very powerful because words said over and over hold power and send a message to Spirit. Make sure you are sending the right message.

Sometimes in this work an image or a set of words adds power to the ingredient you are going to be working with, so keep that in mind. One such product is "20 Mule Team Borax." Can you imagine the power of twenty mules working together for the same goal? They would be unstoppable! Borax is a laundry detergent and a good one. It will not only cleanse your clothes, but it can also be added to washes and baths. You can add it to other ingredients to make an herbal wash, or you can add a small amount directly into the bath. When we are around a lot of folks, our clothes, like our spirits, pick up whatever they are putting out there, so it is important that we keep our clothes as spiritually clean as possible. This is a must for folks who work in hospitals, police officers, attorneys, and anyone else who comes in contact with illness, death, and hostility on a daily basis.

Ammonia

Ammonia is used to strip away things that are holding you back like blocks and crossed conditions. Ammonia is a great cleaner and used in Conjure as a powerful cleanser: to spiritually purify, wash away, and remove crossed conditions, jinxes, and all forms of evil. It is also used as a general cleansing of spiritual energy for altar spaces, homes, and businesses. The only thing is that you have to be careful when working with ammonia because it will strip away the good luck along with the bad. You need to be very light-handed when you use ammonia in blockbuster and uncrossing work.

Black Coffee

Black coffee is like so many other ingredients: it strips things away. When added to a cleansing bath, it will remove anything that is on you. As the elders are passing, information is being lost—like the use of Red Devil Lye—and the use of coffee in conjure work is also being forgotten. A lot of household ingredients are being left out of the teachings for commercial reasons. If you can make your own goods, why would you buy them from a store? If you do make your own products, then those commercial outlets are losing money. The ancestors didn't run to the store every time they needed something; they used what was on hand. Some elders will tell you to use three-day-old coffee. They tell you this because it takes time for the oil to rise on top of the coffee. A strong cup of black coffee will do the same thing.

Bones

The black cat bone is added to works to draw good luck, power, and success in love and money. The other bone that is kind of famous in conjure work is the raccoon penis bone. It is worked as a love charm. It is believed that the bones pick up the animal's traits, so they are very powerful to be added to the work. Opossum bones are good for reading the bones, but they are also good to add to works when the works need to be hidden. The possum is known for its playing dead to throw folks off.

Brooms

Brooms are a big deal in the Southern culture. In my home growing up we were never allowed to play with the broom. If your feet get swept over with the broom in this house, then the first reaction is to get the broom and spit on the head of it. If you don't, then it could draw the law to you. Sweeping behind someone as they leave your home will keep them away. Putting the broom with the head up behind the door will keep unwanted folks from coming over. Placing a broom across the doorway of a bedroom will keep out hags and nightmares. The list just goes on and on of dos and don'ts. The broom is also good for spiritual brush-downs. It is a good cleansing tool and also good for protection of the home.

Chicken Feet

Chicken feet are good for spiritual cleansing. You scratch about an inch from your body starting at the crown of your head going downward. While you are doing this, say the first verse of Psalm 23. Make sure that you do your feet also, going from heel to toe. If you are removing a crossed or jinxed condition, you would do this for nine nights in a row. The wing of a chicken makes a wonderful fan for all types of cleansing and sweepings; it can be worked with like a broom. Chickens peck and scratch and clean the yard all day, so no wonder the foot and wing work so well in cleansing. They will remove jinxed conditions, crossed conditions, or anything else that may have been put on you or that you have attracted.

Eggs

Eggs are good for pulling things off of yourself like blocks, jinxes, cross conditions, and illness. You can cleanse yourself by wiping yourself down with an egg while praying that whatever is on you be pulled off into the egg. It is important that you go in only one direction when doing this type of work. Once you are done with the brush-down, finish the work by cracking the egg in a glass of water. Place two broom straws on top of the glass of water in the shape of a cross so that whatever was pulled off stays in the glass. Dispose of the glass with the water, egg, and broom straws by leaving it at a crossroads or at the base of a tree. An alternative method is, having first brushed yourself down with it, you can throw the egg in the center of the crossroads with five pennies and let the spirit of the crossroads take care of it.

Gunpowder

Gunpowder is a powerful ingredient in any conjure work. Firecrackers are an easy way to add it to your work. You can write a petition on a piece of paper, then wrap the paper around a firecracker. Brush yourself off with the firecracker while praying all blocks be removed and then very carefully light the firecracker. I usually do three of these in a row when the sun is going down. You can also add it to any work to heat the work up.

Hands of the Clock

I was not taught to work by the phases of the moon; I was taught to plant by them but not to work by them. The most my mama ever said about the moon was when she trimmed our hair, and she did that when the moon was growing so our hair would grow. If you want your hair to grow slowly, then you cut it as the moon is going down, but to me this is common sense because you never plant when the moon is going down because the plants won't grow. They will rot in the ground. I was, however, taught to work by the hands of the clock when I am doing my work. I have never waited for the moon to do my work. I work by the clock. If you are trying to remove something, then you do the work when the hands of the clock are going downward. If you are trying to draw something to you, then you do the work when the hands of the clock are moving upward. The same goes for sunrise and sunset: sunrise draws things to you, and sunset removes things away from you. East and west do the same thing: work placed to the east will draw, and work placed to the west will nail things down and remove them.

Lemon

Lemons are worked with for all types of cleansing works, but they can also be used to cross a target up and sour their world. They are like a double-edged sword: on one hand, they can cleanse and protect, then on the other hand, they can cross a target up by souring their life. I would caution you to make sure you are justified in this type of work; a reversal could send it right back to you if they did one and busted the container the work was in. Lemon is used in most cut and clear work.

Lysol (Original Brown)

I love this stuff, and my children can't stand the smell of it! Lysol is a very powerful cleanser, but it also adds protection to the home. It will cut and clear all issues out of the home. When my children were home and their friends were in and out of the house, I would mop at least three times a week because, like I said, folks track stuff into our homes and lives. I learned from my mama to take care of the doorways in the home and to make sure there is nothing brought in that could cause issues within the home. The original Lysol is getting hard to find, so when I do find it, I buy it in bulk. You can also clean your bath-tub with it after a spiritual bath or if there is a lot of fussing in the home. It will clear it out and send it down the drain.

Ms. Stewart's Bluing

Some workers use Blue Balls in some of their work. Blue Balls are not safe, but you can use Ms. Stewart's Bluing and it is just as good. Ms. Stewart's Bluing is easy to find in the store and good for keeping white clothes white and removing any-thing that may have been picked up. It is good for many things in conjure work: You can add a little to a glass of water to draw Spirit into a reading, and it will protect the reader from unwanted spirits. You can place a small glass of water behind the door to protect your home. You can also add a few drops to any protection or cleansing bath to help empower the bath. It is good for protection, cleansings, and luck; it will also bring peace to a home.

Murphy's Oil Soap

Murphy's Oil Soap has lemongrass in it, which is an ingredient in Van Van oil, a famous commercial conjure oil. I wash my walls with this soap twice a year to keep my home healthy and running smooth. It is great for homes and businesses to cut and clear blocks and crossed conditions. A small capful can be added to a spray bottle to spray across the threshhold of the home or of a business to clear away any unwanted things that might have been dropped in the doorway.

Nails

Nails are a must in the working cabinet; the ole-timey square-head nails can be made into a cross and placed at your front and back doors for protection. Old rusty nails are the best ones to work with. Nails are used to nail down a target, your property, a job, and in many other works. They can be used in crossing work as well as healing works; it all depends on the job.

Oak Branches

An oak branch can be used just like a broom to sweep out conditions in the home or around the property. You start from the back of the home or yard and sweep forward using the branch as a broom. You can also brush yourself off with a small oak branch to remove crossed conditions. They are also worked with for power and protection.

Pins & Needles

Pins and needles are worked with in a few different ways. They can be used with a candle where each day the candle is burned on a target and there are pins stuck in the candle. They are used to harm an enemy and can be used to nail a target down. Sometimes they are used in healing to nail down the illness so it can be removed.

Railroad Spikes

These spikes are forged in iron, so they are very powerful. The railroad spike is used for all types of protection conjure. The iron is unbendable so it won't break. Railroad spikes are used in Conjure to nail your land down. They are also good for works to protect your money. You can make protection amulets and place them behind the doors of your home; one could also be made to protect your money or your job. This type of work is called "nailing down."

Red Devil Lye

You can't hardly find Red Devil Lye nowadays, but there are some old feed stores and hardware stores that still carry it. When it was available, conjure workers would advise a client to bury the lye at the four corners of their home with the devil facing outward for protection. There is an old work to keep bill collectors from your door until you can pay what you owe: You need a can of Red Devil Lye, a dime, and the business name with you petition written over the name. You have to be very careful as you add the ingredients into the container of lye. You have to say your prayers and petition as you are loading the work. Then you bury the container to the west where the sun goes down. Eventually they will stop bothering you and give you time to pay the bill. Red Devil Lye is also good to get rid of unwanted people and for enemies. Even just the empty container can be used for these types of works. After all, they will still have the spirit of the lye in them.

Salt

Salt is a powerhouse! Salt guarantees our blessings, preservation, and protection under God. Salt is also like a double-edged sword: it can bless and curse. Do you remember Lot's wife who was turned into a statue of salt? Salt will hold prayers and petitions—that is one of the reasons it is so powerful. It can also cut away cross conditions like the blade of a knife.

Saltpeter

Saltpeter is used for uncrossing, blockbuster, and crossing works and works to tie a man's nature, which means to stop a man from wanting or being able to have sex. My own mama used it on my daddy, and I know this for a fact. I asked her what it was, and she said, "your daddy's medicine." I was twenty-five at the time. My oldest sister told me what it was for, so trust me, I have never forgotten that day. It can be added to blockbusting and road-opening washes. Some folks still use it in spiritual baths. This is old Conjure at its best.

Scissors

Scissors are another tool in Conjure the use of which is being lost to this new age group of workers coming up. Scissors cut conjure work thrown against you; you can keep a pair opened on the door frame of the front of your house. They will cut away anything folks try to bring into your home, and they will keep unwanted spirits and work out of the home. There are rules about scissors: you should never point scissors at someone you love because they will cut the bond between you. Scissors are used to cut away illness and crossed conditions; they are also used for protection.

Sulfur

We have sulfur around us every day if we use matches in our homes. The ole folks say the strike of a match will send the devil running. Sulfur is one of the main ingredients in work where you are trying to run a spirit out of your home or when you have serious blocks or illnesses in the home. Sulfur is also one of the ingredients in hotfoot powder and some types of crossing powders. You will find that some ingredients can either cure or curse, and sulfur is another one of those double-edged ingredients. It is added to all enemy work, hotfoot powders, as well as crossing conjure and some blockbusting works as well as run devil run works. A pinch of sulfur behind the door will help protect the home from cross conditions and false friends.

Vinegar

An all-around spiritual cleanser, vinegar can be added to mop water as well as spiritual baths. A wash made of vinegar and holy water can be used to pour over the head to cut away any confusion or crossed conditions. If you decide to try the wash, it is equal parts of vinegar and holy water. You will need to wrap your head in a white cloth for ten minutes as the hands of the clock are going downward. When the ten minutes are up, you can wash your hair. Then wrap it up in a white cloth for another ten minutes as the hands of the clock move upward; then dress your crown of your head with some type of spiritual oil. This wash is good for your spirit and your head; it helps strip away product buildup on your scalp and helps control dry scalp, all the while helping to cut and clear blocks.

WHAT'S HIDDEN

THERE ARE MANY WORKS hidden within the culture that this work comes from. I imagine some folks don't even realize what they are doing; they simply do it because their mama or grandma or some elder aunt did it that way. They don't have a name for it because there were no labels put on it. The labels came with the internet and the work being put out there for the entire world to know. But the problem is that what is put out there is a half-baked cake; a lot of the ingredients are missing. Here's a small example of what I am talking about. My favorite auntie taught me to sew when I was little. She sewed for the public, and every year she would make my school clothes for me. I could describe what I wanted, and she would make the pattern for it. One thing she did that I questioned her about was on every hem she sewed she would make three knots at the beginning and three at the end when she was tying off the hem. One day I asked her why she did that; she didn't know. It was the way my great grandma had taught her to sew, and that is the way she had always done it and that is the way she taught me to do it.

It would be many years later that I would find out what the three knots represent and why you tie them at the beginning and the end of a job. My aunt didn't consider herself a conjure woman; she did things because that is what she was taught. Southern children are taught not to question an elder, so I doubt she quizzed my great grandma on why you tie three knots. That would have been very disrespectful. Years later when I was taught how to make packets and conjure bags, I was told about the three knots. The three knots represent the Holy Trinity: God the Father, God the Son, and God the Holy Spirit. If my auntie knew that, she didn't share it with me, but that's the way the culture is. You're taught to do something a certain way and there is no asking questions or wanting to know why. You just do what you are told and how you are told to do it.

The broom and sweeping were another big deal in my family. I saw children using the broom for a horse and playing with the broom. Growing up we were not allowed to do that. I grew up with the rule that the broom was not to be played with, and you didn't sweep folks feet with the broom. If you did, then they needed to spit on the head of the broom. My grandma and mama didn't explain why; that is just how it was. You should never watch someone you love leave the house and then sweep behind them out the door. If you do, you could sweep them out of your life. I learned later on in life why not to do it. My mama just taught us not to; she never explained why. My grandma is the one that taught me how to really sweep with a broom. She was tough as nails, and I got switched a few times on my legs for not sweeping the yard right but I finally got it after a few switchings. You had to sweep in long strokes going forward. You should never sweep back and forth with a broom. Again, I didn't learn why until I was much older. Sweeping back and forth just stirs up mess and doesn't move anything out. By sweeping forward in long strokes, you are moving things away from you. I surely didn't ask her why I had to sweep that way. If I think hard on it, I can still see her standing in the backyard schooling me on how to sweep the yard.

These are conjure-related things that folks do every day in my culture and don't know why they do them. The work is hidden throughout the culture. It is taught when you are growing up. You live it daily. That is why this work is so important to me. It's not something I do; it is my whole life. It's all I know, and it is how I live and how I have raised my family and how they are raising theirs. It is a little different because, unlike my people, I tell them why something needs to be done a certain way. There are four living generations as of this book, and each one of them except G-baby, my great granddaughter, knows and understands their culture and the work because they grew up in it. When G-baby is old enough to understand, she will be taught too. I haven't studied this. I live it every day of my life.

Here is another thing that is hidden but a lot of rural Southern folks still use and that is turpentine. When I was a child, every year we had to take a dose of turpentine and sugar to kill worms. This is what some folks call "live things in you"; that is where that comes from. The turpentine was supposed to kill tapeworms and pinworms. Sweet Jesus, I hated that stuff, but my mama dosed us faithfully every year with it. She didn't hide why we had to take it. We knew exactly what it was for.

She used to clean out shoes with turpentine, which I now know cleansed away anything that we might have picked up. We were never allowed to wear our shoes in the house. Every Saturday growing up, we had to wash the porch and the front stoop. My friends thought my mama was weird for making us wash them. I still wash my stoop and my breezeway.

I want to share one more little tidbit before I move on. Lots of folks throw mothballs under their house and in their yards; most will say it is to keep snakes away or it's just something they were taught. Did you know that mothballs will cut jinxes and conditions thrown in your yard? They should be buried on the four corners of the property, the four corners of the house, placed under the house and buried by the front and back door. This is more hidden Conjure that folks don't realize they are working. They simply do it because that is what someone taught them to do.

There are many works and teachings hidden in the stories like Brer Rabbit and the Old Testament and in the little things children are taught to do. All of this comes from the ancestors. They were treated as slaves and had no rights. Everything that they did had to be hidden, even their emotions. That is why Southern folks don't usually act out in public; it is kept for private meetings. In order to really understand this work, you truly have to understand the whole culture. The ancestors of this work had to keep everything secret, so the work became a daily routine like the way to sweep, the way to sew, the way to treat your children—all these things make up this work and are an important part of it. To just do the magic part of it is whitewashing it and diluting it. You are also insulting the spirits of the ancestors who died during slavery and who were maimed and tormented. You have to look beyond the work or spells as some folks call it; you need to look deep and pay attention to what you are looking at because you never know what may be hidden there. I wanted to leave you here and move on, but I have one more thing to share.

Here is a bit of conjure work I bet most have never heard of. In the ole days there were elders who treated trees. There are still some alive today if you can find them. When Hurricane Rita hit Texas, she destroyed one of our large pecan trees and damaged the other one. I thought we were gonna lose it too. Folks who treat trees don't advertise. You won't find them in the yellow pages like ole workers. To find them you gotta know someone who knows someone until you reach them. I was determined not to lose this tree so I started asking around. Finally a friend of mine new of an ole guy but wasn't sure if he was still alive or not. I went looking for him and found him. I also got a lesson in treating trees or, I should say, conjuring trees.

He came to our home right as the sun was going down. I just thought it was because it was cooling that time of day, but that isn't why. And yes, I asked a lot of questions. He needed to see where the shadow of the branches on the tree stopped; he told us that is where the end of the roots of the tree is. All he had was a big hammer and iron spikes; that's it. He nailed three nails on the outer shadow, then three around the base of the tree and one in the tree. I asked him why he was using iron spikes, and he said because the iron will feed the tree. Now in my mind as a conjure worker, I also understood that he was nailing the spirit of the tree down so it couldn't leave the tree. There are a lot of works in Conjure where nails are used in trees to help or hinder a target. I am happy to say that it seemed like the treatment wouldn't help, but in the end it did and the tree is once more growing.

He was taught how to treat trees by his daddy, so it was something passed on from one generation to the other. There are touches of Conjure in it, and I don't doubt that he moved here as a young child from Savannah. Once again there was something hidden and something learned. Below you will find a work that I have shared often because I know it really works. You can find out things that are hidden by calling on the Prophet Daniel to help open your eyes so you can really see what you are overlooking.

I CAN SEE CLEARLY NOW

Call on the Trinity, the ancestors, and then the Prophet Daniel in order to do this work. In Daniel 2 V 22 we see that God reveals things that are hidden.

DANIEL 2 V 22

22 HE REVEALS DEEP AND SECRET THINGS; HE KNOWS WHAT IS IN THE DARKNESS, AND LIGHT DWELLS WITH HIM.

I watched my mama many times looking in a cup or a glass with water in it. Sometimes it was clear water; sometimes it had a blue tint to it. I never asked her what she was doing. When she was in what we called "her Mood," we didn't mess with her. My mama never burned candles; I do because I love them. She would just sit there gazing into the water. I often wondered as a child what she was looking at.

If you need to find what is being hidden from you, then petition the Prophet Daniel to help you see what it is. When there is something hidden in the dark that you just can't put your finger on, get a jar or glass of water. I use an ole mason jar. Add a few drops of Ms. Stewart's Bluing to the water, along with a little holy water. Get a white stick candle and place it behind the jar or glass. Petition God and the Prophet Daniel to help you find the answer you are looking for. Ask them to help you see what is hidden.

I leave my jar on my table in my shop. I don't let the water dry up; if the water gets low, I just add more water and stir it up. This is an ole-school way of reading. If you haven't ever tried it, you should.

DRAWIN' & REMOVIN'

THERE ARE A SET of works within Conjure that can either draw things to you or remove things from you. These types of works are known by a few different names.

* Attraction work is done to draw things into your life that you need, money drawing work, success work, and other works of these types are worked to draw.

* Reversal work, cleansing works, and cut and clear works are all done to remove something from your life.

You need to have a good understanding of both of these types of works before you decide to do them. You may be thinking, "Well, attraction works are simply drawing what I need and want into my life." Let's get real: nothing is ever that simple in life. If you are having to do attraction work, then there are things going on in your life that are causing issues. If you simply do attraction work, then you are just patching the underlying issue, which will still be there when the attraction work runs out. Some folks have called me an expert in this work. I am nobody's expert. I have learned through the years what and what not to do. My mama used to say, "a hard head makes a soft behind." We all have to learn our lessons.

Drawing and removing work go hand in hand. If you have to do one type of work, then you really need to follow up with the other type of work. If you have to do a cut and clear work to remove something or someone from your life, then you need to do some type of drawing work to fill that void with something you want or need in your life. You could just do nothing, but something is going to fill that void left in your spirit. This type of work is not modern. Back in the days of the ancestors these works were born out of necessity. Some of them were worked with for healing as well as crossing. They used what they had, and most of them always had Irish potatoes. There is a work my mama used on us if we were sick or hurting somewhere. Of course, as children we didn't pay much attention to what she was doing, but as I got older, I watched her like a hawk. To me there was nothing my mama couldn't fix.

This is a simple work to remove something or someone from your life. You simply need an Irish potato. If you are trying to remove an illness, then you rub the potato over the affected area going in a downward motion. You can even set the potato on the area while praying that whatever is there be moved into the potato. Then you bury the potato on the west side of the house as the sun is setting. Then just forget about it; as the potato rots away, so will the illness be gone. Nowadays when folks want to remove someone from their life, the first thing most do is hotfoot. Hotfoot work should be the last thing you do; if nothing else works and the situation is dire, then do hotfoot. Hotfoot has been made popular over the internet, but that type of work is harmful and shouldn't be done just because you don't like someone or they made you mad. You have to remember that this work is all about justice and being a justified worker. Here is a work that can be done in a couple of different ways—to stop gossip and to move someone away from you without hotfoot.

To shut someone's mouth who can't seem to mind their own business, you need an Irish potato and red pepper. Using a sharp knife, you need to cut a piece of the potato deep into the center. Save the piece you cut out because that is what you will use to plug the hole you made in the potato back up after you have loaded the potato. Like most old works, this is so simple you wonder how powerful it really is. Trust me, it works and it works well. Once you have the hole made in the potato, name the potato for the target just like you would if you were making a dollie. Tell the target that every time they talk about you or yours, their mouth will become sore and burn like fire. Put the red pepper in the hole you made in the potato and plug it up. Then bury the potato on the west side on the corner of the house when the sun is rising, because this is what you want to bring to the target every time they gossip about you. You want their mouth to burn like it is on fire, and at the same time by burying them in the west corner of the house, you are removing them from your life. This is called a double action work.

To drive someone away, you need an Irish potato and the dirt from a crossroads away from you. Using a sharp knife, you need to cut a piece of the potato deep into the center. Save the piece you cut out because that is what you will use to plug the hole you made in the potato back up after you have loaded the potato. Name the potato after the target and then load the dirt from the crossroads into the potato and plug the hole up. Now there are two ways you can do this job, and either one of them will work well. You can bury the potato on the west side on the corner of the house when the sun is setting, or you can take the potato to running water and throw it in. Either way, the target will be removed from you. This work is all about working with what you have in your home. You don't have to buy a bunch of supplies to get a job done. I have added some other works below to help you get started with removing the old and drawing in the new.

LOVE YOURSELF POWER WORK

If you are coming out of a bad relationship or if you have been hurt deeply, then you need to do some work on yourself before you try to draw a new love into your life. You need to do some spiritual cleansing on yourself to heal your spirit. You don't want to draw that same type of person to yourself or carry old baggage into a brand-new relationship. Cleansing work is very important before you start any kind of attraction or love work. This work not only helps you cleanse away all the pain and hurt, but it also helps you build your personal power. You need a plate that has been cleansed with running water and dressed with some type of holy oil, a white handkerchief, one tealight, a photo of yourself, a blue candle, lovage root, Solomon's seal, Master of the Woods, calamus root, frankincense, myrrh, lavender, and some powdered sugar.

Set the plate and candle off to the side and lay out your hankie, take a pinch of each one of the ingredients one at the time, pray your petition over them, and place them on the hankie on your altar. Take the tealight and dress it with your oil. Set the tealight on top of your ingredients and pray your petition over it. Let the tealight burn completely out. While the tealight is working, take a photo of yourself and write your petition for personal power across your photo. Set your photo on top of your plate. Once the tealight has burned out, take the blue candle and starting at the crown of your head, wipe downward to the bottom of your feet. Repeat this a few times and really focus on cleansing your head. Blue is a healing color; it also calms and soothes the spirit. When you have finished the cleansing with the candle, set the candle on top of your photo.

Sprinkle your ingredients around the photo going with the hands of the clock while praying your petition. Light your blue vigil candle and pray your petition over your work along with these power words "The Lord is my Shepherd, I shall not want. . . ." Try to pray your petition over the work at least three times. Once the candle burns out, take the photo and the ingredients off the plate and tie them up in the white handkerchief. Pray your petition for personal power into the packet and feed it whatever oil you feel is appropriate at least once a week. Keep your packet on you.

REVERSAL WORK

JEREMIAH 16 V 16–18

16 "BUT NOW I WILL SEND FOR MANY FISHERMEN," DECLARES THE LORD, "AND THEY WILL CATCH THEM. AFTER THAT I WILL SEND FOR MANY HUNTERS, AND THEY WILL HUNT THEM DOWN ON EVERY MOUNTAIN AND HILL AND FROM THE CREVICES OF THE ROCKS.

17 MY EYES ARE ON ALL THEIR WAYS; THEY ARE NOT HIDDEN FROM ME, NOR IS THEIR SIN CONCEALED FROM MY EYES.

18 I WILL REPAY THEM DOUBLE FOR THEIR WICKEDNESS AND THEIR SIN, BECAUSE THEY HAVE DEFILED MY LAND WITH THE LIFELESS FORMS OF THEIR VILE IMAGES AND HAVE FILLED MY INHERITANCE WITH THEIR DETESTABLE IDOLS."

Some of you might be wondering what a reversal is. A reversal is a set of conjure works that removes whatever condition is on a person and returns it back to the sender. I think there is a misconception about reversal work: some folks think that if you do reversal work you are crossing the person up. This is absolutely not true! You are removing whatever has been sent to you right back to the sender; if they get knocked on their ass, that is all on them. You are only taking off what they have sent to you.

Another misconception is that folks think that cleansing and reversal work are the same work. This is also absolutely not true. Let me explain. While they both do remove crossed conditions, they don't both return the said condition to the sender. Cleansing work does just that: it removes the blocks and any other cross condition that is on a person. Reversal work not only removes the crossed condition, but it also gives the sender a taste of their own medicine. There is a kind of safety clause in reversal work: if the work was justified, then nothing will happen to the person who did the work. Meaning if you deserved the issues you are having through your own action, then the worker is safe from any reversal work. On the other hand, if you are innocent, then the worker will feel the justice served by the spirits. It's kind of like a double-edged sword: dull on the side of the innocent and razor sharp on the side of the guilty! I have written up a few Q&As that I hope will answer some of readers' questions about reversal work. The main thing to remember is that when reversal work is done, it will only hit those who justly deserve it; the innocent will not be harmed by the work.

Q&A

Q. How do I know if I need to keep the reversal going?

A. Here are a few other symptoms that you may be feeling if you need to do a reversal work and keep it going:

* Confusion
* Sleep too much or sleep too little

* Light-headedness
* Money blocks
* Disaster everywhere you turn that just keeps happening
* Sickness that doesn't go away
* You feel like someone's watching or sitting on your chest when you're asleep.

I could go on and on but I think you get the idea.

Q. How often can I do a reversal?

A. You can do reversal work anytime you feel you have a crossed condition or you feel someone has put blocks up around you.

Q. Will the work come back on me?

A. This is another myth. As long as you are justified in your work, then you are safe.

Q. Will reversal work start a spiritual war?

A. The answer is absolutely not because you are only returning what has been sent to you. If they were justified in crossing you up, then no reversal in the world is going to harm them, but if they were unjustified, then they're going to get their own medicine right back in their lap. Think of it as an undeliverable package at the post office and stamp it with RETURN TO SENDER.

Q. How do I keep crossed conditions off me?

A. The way to keep folks from being able to cross you up is to keep your protections up. You also need to set up routine cleansings and reversals.

Q. What is justified work?

A. When you hear a worker say they will only do justified work, just exactly what are they talking about? Justified work is done when the target deserves it. That is why reversal work is the best way to go. You don't just work on someone because they pissed you off. When a worker jumps the gun and just starts throwing because someone made them mad, this shows an immature worker who needs to go back and learn the ethics of Conjure 101. If I worked like this, I'd never get any rest.

When you decide to work on someone, you really need to have a valid reason. This work was not meant to be thrown around on a whim; it can be dangerous. Let me give you a few examples of justified work. If a child is harmed, this calls for justified work. If a woman is battered, it's justified work. If money is owed: justified work. If a neighbor won't leave you alone: justified work. So you get the idea? Justified work should fit the crime. Do not throw at someone because they pissed you off. If you do and they do a reversal, then you will get hit with your own work plus theirs. Like my daughter says, "Use your thinker not your stinker"—meaning don't be an ass, think before you react! Always be smarter and work with a cool head.

Reversal work is usually done with a candle that has two different colors. The colors will be black and white, green and black, black and red, or orange and black. Most people think that the black and white candle is the best candle to use for a crossed condition, the red and black for a love jinx, a green and black for a money block, and orange and black will help bring change into your life. I personally prefer the black and red one for all my reversal work. The red and black one always works well for me. The other colors are hard to find, but you can find a red and black one almost anywhere they sell this type of candle.

The black in the candle pulls off anything that doesn't belong on your spirit, and the red represents the blood. If you want to bring about changes within your life, then you need to work with an orange and black stick candle. Orange is powerful because it draws and it gives you control. You should always do what feels right for you, so if you are not sure about where to start with reversals, then I highly recommend using a red and black stick candle.

I have been asked how often you should do a reversal. The answer is it all depends on your situation. If you have a lot of things going on in your life, then you may want to do a set of reversals. Let's face it, not everyone is gonna love you, and when you are dealing with folks who are envious, jealous, or just don't like you nowadays, you don't know what to do. Everybody is a worker, so what do you do? *Reversal* work! If you are in the public eye or around a lot of folks daily, I suggest you do a reversal at least once a month. If things seem to be going bad, then I'd do one once a week until things settled down. You also need to remember to keep your protections up at all times; this will help.

I'm gonna give you a couple of reversal works that you can work with. Always do what feels right to you. Remember a reversal candle should never be dressed with anything, you don't want to fill it up with oil and such, as it needs to be filled with what it pulls off of you.

Ole-School Reversal Work

This reversal work is two steps, and you will be working with stick candles; one black and one red. This is an ole-school work from days gone by before there were glass candles.

You need a black stick candle. You place the black stick candle at the crown of your head, then start to wipe yourself down
going all the way to your feet, and then you wipe from heel
to toe. Always remember to wipe your head, the back of your
neck, your shoulders, chest, hands, and feet thoroughly with
the black candle because these are the areas when you are hit
the hardest with crossed conditions.

As you are wiping yourself down, pray to your higher power
that all blocks in your life are immediately removed and returned
to sender. Pray that justice is served and they get a taste of their
own medicine.

In the next part of the work you will do the opposite with
the red stick candle. You start at the bottom of your feet and
wipe upwards until you reach the crown of your head. While
you are doing this, you pray and petition the Trinity and the
ancestors to draw the things you need into your life. The red
stick candle will draw to you whatever was taken away or lost
because of the crossed conditions. After you bring the candle
up to your crown, then take a nail and write your birth name
on the candle, dress the candle with holy oil, light the candle,
then place it on top of your photo. Sprinkle a little Master of
the Woods, powdered sugar, and angelica root around the red
candle. Pray for success, love, and happiness.

To destroy another worker throwing roots on you, use the
whole chapter of Isaiah 47 to defeat them. It cancels out any
works done in your name and blinds them so they cannot use
divination nor spirits to "see" you. Tear out chapter 47, write
"all my enemies" on it, and load it into a doll baby. Isaiah 47
works like a triple-edged sword because it crosses them up with
their own work where your enemies can't uncross themselves
nor have anyone help them. It also stops them and anyone
helping them from putting curses on you.

Coffee Bath

This will help remove any blocks that may be holding you back.

You need to take five coffee baths and pray Isaiah 41 and Psalm 23 daily. Make sure you dress yourself with some type of holy oil after each bath.

Here's the recipe for the bath:

1 cup strong black coffee

4 tablespoons table salt

1 cap lemon juice

Pray Isaiah 54 V 17 daily.

Isaiah 54 V 17

17 No weapon that is formed against thee shall prosper; and every tongue that shall rise against thee in judgment thou shalt condemn. This is the heritage of the servants of the LORD, and their righteousness is of me, saith the LORD.

Red Onion Reversal Work

The red onion can draw love, money, prosperity, or whatever you need because it is sweet, but it is also bitter, which makes it good for cleansing and uncrossing work. If your home is in an uproar, you can cleanse yourself and your home with a red onion. This will help stop all the fussing and arguing. This works because the onion is considered bitter. The onion will pull any negative energy in your home into itself. It can also be worked to sweeten your relationship. Because they are both sweet and bitter, they can serve a dual purpose like the ole saying "killing two birds with one stone." This type of job is considered a double action work because you are removing and drawing at the same time.

To do this work, you'll need a new broom, large red onion, some whiskey, a large glass bowl, a photo of you and your target, pyrite, a coin given to you by your target, lovage, salt, sugar, Master of the Woods, spikenard, a small pinch of gunpowder, frankincense and myrrh, a magnet, and some honey. Hold the red onion to your mouth, call on the Trinity and your ancestors, and ask Spirit to cleanse and sweeten your relationship. Hold the broom to your mouth, call on the Trinity and your ancestors, and pray your petition asking them to sweep away all blocks and troubles affecting your home. Sprinkle a few drops of whiskey on the broom head to feed the Spirit. Use the broom to sweep the onion through the house while praying that all blocks be removed. The broom will help sweep out all the buildup in your home and your relationship that is causing the problems. By working this way, you are doubling up the power of your prayers; this is another reason why this is considered a double action work.

Core the center out of the onion, then place it in the large bowl. Write your petition on top of the photo; keep it simple. Burn the photo to ash; then put the ash, the pyrite, the coin, lovage to draw love into the relationship, a pinch of salt prayed over for protection, sugar to sweeten him, Master of the Woods so you have the upper hand, spikenard so things run smoothly, then add a tiny pinch of gunpowder to heat the work up. Don't get heavy-handed with the gunpowder; too much can cause a breakup. Add the frankincense and myrrh to add power to the work and to bless the home. Tear off five small pieces of broom straw from the broom. Add the straws to the onion to keep the devils out of your home. Clean the magnet under running water, then give the magnet a drink of whiskey. Call on the Trinity and your ancestors and pray your petition over the magnet; pray that all crossed conditions be removed from your relationship. Don't feed the magnet anything other than a taste of whiskey because the magnet will feed itself by pulling all blocks out of your relationship. Place the magnet in the onion with the other ingredients. Add a few drops of whiskey in the onion to give the work added power. Pour some of the honey over the onion to cover the onion in its sweetness.

Place the bowl on your love altar; you will be making a cross setup using white candles. Then you will place a tealight on top of the work. You need to call on the Trinity and your ancestors, then one at the time, pick up a candle and pray your petition into it. Pray your petition three times into the candle. When you say your petition over something three times, you're locking the work down. This way the work can't be undone. Place the first candle at the top of your setup, the second one to the bottom, the third to the right, and the last one to the left with the tealight on the top of the onion. Light them the same way you placed them: top to bottom, then right to left, then the one on top of the work. The cross setup represents the crossroads with Holy Spirit in the middle to empower your work.

When the candles burn out, mix some powdered sugar, Master of the Woods, and lovage root together. Then get you a large jar. Make a bed of the ingredients in the jar, call on the Trinity and ancestors, then pray your petition into the jar. Then place the onion in the jar. Pray your petition again over the jar, then pour the rest of the ingredients over the onion and cover it with honey. Once again hold the jar up to your mouth and pray your petition into the jar. Close the jar and place it on your love altar. Burn a tealight on the jar daily while praying your petition. This is called working the jar. Shake the jar at least three times while praying your petition. This will keep the work moving; if you just let the jar sit there, then the work will just sit there.

I usually prefer to work with either sugar or syrup for my sweetening work because they work a lot faster than honey, which crystalizes over time and will slow the work down or stop the work completely. One of the reasons for using honey in this work is because honey runs slow when you pour it. It also soothes, and honey is well known for its healing properties. Honey can be used as a preservative too. By adding honey to your work, it will help preserve the onion and keep it from rotting. Honey's soothing effect will help keep things running smoothly. I know this seems like a lot of work, but nothing is free in this life. If you want something, you have to work for it!

AFRICANIZED

THE DAY THE FIRST ANCESTOR was captured and brought onto American soil in 1619 America changed. I know there were indentured servants in America before 1619, but that is not the same as being a slave. The indentured servant would eventually be freed when they paid their debt.

First the Indians were enslaved, but then came the ancestors from Africa. They were not all captured from the same tribe, so you had a mixture of folks. Some of them were enemies, but slavery drew them together. They had a lot to deal with on top of being held like animals.

From the beginning, they were a strong people. Can you imagine what it would feel like to be set up on a platform and have folks checking you out from head to toe, checking your teeth, your private areas, in front of hundreds? The humiliation they had to feel. They endured that and so much more. These are the peoples that this work comes from. You can't claim the work without giving honor to them. I'm not an expert or a researcher; I am simply stating the facts as they are plain and simple: no ancestors, no work period, because it wouldn't have existed.

Folks tend to just bypass the ancestors of this work, and I'm not sure why. Maybe it's because of slavery and how a powerful people were treated, or maybe they feel they have a right to the work. Only they know the truth. For me it's because this is all I know, this is my culture. I have learned that folks are gonna do whatever they feel is their right to do. I'm not here to preach to them; I'm here to share information that may help someone. I first saw the word "Africanized" on Robert Lucas's Facebook page, so thank you, Robert. Robert is a worker and a teacher. The word really says a lot about the ancestors, the church, and the work. Back in the day white folks' worship was a lot different than the worship of the ancestors. The white folks were afraid of the drums and the open way the ancestors tried to worship. Folks fear what they don't understand, so the ancestors were not allowed to worship the way they did in their homeland of Africa. So they did what any intelligent people would do and hid it within a religion they were allowed to practice.

I have to say these white folks put a lot of stock in the Bible and how they thought it would bend folks to their will. The only thing is they were outsmarted even in a time of bondage. They forced the Bible and a religion on folks who made it work for them. They used their knowledge from their homeland and gathered new knowledge from the Bible and made it work. They Africanized the meetinghouse, or prayer house as some call it. It was the only place they could gather and worship. Drums weren't allowed. That was ok 'cause they clapped their hands and stomped their feet for drums. They had their sticks so those took the place of the drums too. They called Spirit into their worship through spirituals and the movements from their homeland. They learned the Bible and the words of wisdom in it, and they turned it around to work for them. The "ring shout" is a perfect example of how they Africanized Christianity to suit them.

During the ring shout folks move in the opposite direction of the clock—this is the direction a worker would work in for reversal works—and they stomp their feet as they move and pray out loud. Shouting is really praying around the altar together. When I was young and going to church, there was a place in the front of the church where folks gathered to pray together and to draw down Spirit. So even though religion was forced on them, they turned it around to work for them. There is a big difference between the AMC church worships and the way mainstream white churches worship. Just like there is a big difference between mainstream Christians and Christians who are conjure workers or rootworkers, whichever label you use to identify what you do. I follow my mama's lead and mind my own business and let other folks mind theirs. All I care about is this work and my culture.

For years folks have tried to make claims that the Bible has nothing to do with this work, but that is simply not true. The ancestors were forced to learn the Bible, and so they put it to good use. To try to remove it now would change the work, and Conjure or hoodoo or whatever word you choose to use would become something else. If you want to really learn about the ancestors and the culture, go to the Gullah Nation. The Gullah people are descendants of the slaves that were brought over here. You can find them along the coast of Georgia and South Carolina. You can try to speak with the elders, and then you will see where the power of this work came from. As my grandson says, "Ya gonna learn something," for they are as close as you can get to the ancestors. As far as I am concerned, the ancestors gave a lot more than they got, and to try and tear this work apart because it doesn't suit folks is just plan disrespectful to these ancestors and the elders who have come after them. Learn the culture, honor the ancestors of this work, and do the work. This work will enhance your life, and by honoring the ancestors, you are in turn honoring yourself. Anytime we show honor and respect to the ancestors, their light shines down on us and we are well gifted for our respect and the honor shown them.

ABOUT THE AUTHOR

STARR CASAS, a veteran Rootworker and traditional Conjure woman, has been helping people for over thirty-five years through her ancestral art of Old Style Conjure. She is one of the preeminent modern masters of this southern American style of folk magic, and she maintains an active teaching schedule. Starr is also among the organizers of the annual New Orleans Folk Magic Festival. Visit her at *www.oldstyleconjure.com.*

HOUDINI, THE CONJURE ROOSTER

TO OUR READERS

Weiser Books, an imprint of Red Wheel/Weiser, publishes books across the entire spectrum of occult, esoteric, speculative, and New Age subjects. Our mission is to publish quality books that will make a difference in people's lives without advocating any one particular path or field of study. We value the integrity, originality, and depth of knowledge of our authors.

Our readers are our most important resource, and we appreciate your input, suggestions, and ideas about what you would like to see published.

Visit our website at *www.redwheelweiser.com* to learn about our upcoming books and free downloads, and be sure to go to *www.redwheelweiser.com/newsletter* to sign up for newsletters and exclusive offers.

You can also contact us at *info@rwwbooks.com* or at
Red Wheel/Weiser, LLC
65 Parker Street, Suite 7
Newburyport, MA 01950